GAELEN'S STORY

WILLIAM K SANDIFORD

To Eva

with Best Wishes !

Bill

x

ASHRIDGE PRESS

Published and distributed by
Ashridge Press
A subsidiary of Country Books

ISBN 1 901214 23 0

Design, typesetting and production:
Country Books, Courtyard Cottage, Little Longstone,
Bakewell, Derbyshire DE45 1NN

Tel/Fax: 01629 640670
e-mail: dickrichardson@country-books.co.uk

Printed and bound by: Antony Rowe Ltd.

DEDICATION

I am grateful to Ruth, my wife, for her patience, good counsel... and for so much more.

My thoughts are with the Dead; with them
I live in long-past years,
Their virtues love, their faults condemn,
Partake their hopes and fears,
And from their lessons seek and find
Instruction with a humble mind.

Robert Southey (1774-1843)

CHAPTER 1

It had rained all night, but the clouds had dispersed leaving a boundless expanse of clear sky and a tremendous sense of space. The blueness from above was mirrored in the vast sweep of the Solway Firth, its surface rippling and sparkling under the midday sun. Standing on the quayside at the Isle of Whithorn, I felt the freshness of the sea breeze and tasted its salty air.

Scanning the shoreline of the small and almost circular harbour, I could imagine the scene as it would have appeared a century ago. From this spot, along with scores of other holidaymakers, I might have boarded a steam ferry for the voyage of a lifetime. Rallying to the sound of the ship's horn we'd have sailed westwards around the Mull of Galloway, then north to Arran and on to the Western Isles.

It was quiet now; just a few small yachts moored behind the breakwater, their halyards slapping gently against carbon fibre masts.

I thought about the legend of St Ninian, the man who'd brought Christianity to Galloway in AD400. He'd built his tiny chapel at Whithorn just three miles away... the first stone building in Scotland, according to some.

I recalled the cave which still bears his name, situated by the seashore at the southernmost point of this peninsular known locally as the Machars. I'd taken Hilary and our two children to see St Ninian's cave some days ago, at the beginning of our holiday. It was said to be the place where he'd gone to think, and to plan his missionary work. Even now I could recall those strong winds ripping clouds of salt-laden mist from the surface of the sea, the breakers crashing down at the cave's entrance, and the loud clattering of pebbles as first they were driven up the steep shore, only to be drawn back beneath each retreating wave.

That cave, and St Ninian's shrine at Whithorn, had been places of pilgrimage for kings, queens and countless other Christian mortals for centuries. Ninian must have loved the sea, the green pastureland with its silver-grey outcrops of rock, and those glorious heather-topped hills to the north. Gazing out across the Solway Firth towards the southern horizon, my eyes rested on the hazy outline of the Isle of Man. A thin layer of cloud hovered above its crest... another familiar sight to St Ninian, perhaps.

These few days with my family had passed too quickly. I'd begun to lose touch with the world of organised work, but thoughts of returning to the rat race were already destroying my peace of mind. I'd begun to experience a new sense of longing... surely there had to be more.

I heard Hilary's voice, sharp and clear some way behind me, and glanced round. She'd been watching over Anna and Michael fishing for crabs off the harbour wall. Now she was heading towards me, looking down at the ground and speaking into the mobile phone, her pace quickening as she moved closer.

"Yes, he's here at the quayside... his last chance for some fresh air and sanity before he gets back. Just one moment..." She handed me the phone, and her face said it all; my peace was about to be overturned, my sense of tranquillity mutilated.

"It's someone at your wretched office," she whispered. "He's very apologetic, or says he is; thought it best to ring you now, apparently."

"Hi... this is Richard Dunstan speaking!" I tried to sound sprightly and businesslike, as if already back at the office and ready to face any challenge.

But my mind was in turmoil. Why contact me now, whilst I was still on holiday? Had one of my team leaders suddenly resigned? That was it! Simmering resentment at having been passed-over for promotion... it was bound to happen eventually. Some of the section managers were older and more experienced than me, yet I'd been promoted to lead the group. It had been an uphill struggle over the passed six months just to keep the dialogue going. Or was there something else? Had something gone wrong with one of my projects?

I listened in silence as the tale of woe unfolded. It had all started before coming away on holiday. I'd been told to prepare a bid for some new work, and having worked long hours and stayed up all night to find ways of reducing the costs, I'd left it behind as a draft. But during my absence the bid had been turned into a contract proposal and sent to the customer. Everyone had signed-up to it, and now our managing director wanted to know how I'd arrived at those costs.

In effect, I'd been used as a gambling pawn by the senior management team. Success in winning the contract would open up the chance of even more work. But failure to achieve deadlines would shatter my credibility. I'd seen it happen to others. There were always plenty of newly qualified engineers lining up for jobs like mine, and they were cheaper to employ.

"Oh, and just one other thing, Richard...!" There was something devious and underhand about his tone of voice, and I felt those familiar palpitations in my chest as the sea breeze turned cold. "You didn't know about the quality inspection, did you? Your guys are being quality-audited next week. It's a big one, Richard... the company's accreditation could depend on it... just a little something for you to think about over the weekend!"

I rang-off, and turned back to face the sea.

"Don't even imagine it," Hilary whispered, moving closer and linking her arm into mine.

"Imagine what?"

"Escaping to the Isle of Man... it's a good twenty miles... thirty to Ramsay. You wouldn't make it before nightfall."

"I might... in a sea kayak. That's how the Celts would have done it."

"The Celts...?" she laughed. "Since when did a Celt need to be back in time for work on a Monday morning?" And then, squeezing my arm, "Anyway, you'd need to turn some of this into *real* muscle first. With those tidal currents you'd most probably end up in Iceland."

I'd had my doubts about coming all this way to Scotland, and she knew it. But what she hadn't realised, and what I couldn't so easily admit to, was my growing lack of enthusiasm for taking any kind of annual holiday. The longer I was away from work, the more likely it seemed that some crisis or another would arise in my absence. Not a healthy attitude; but that's how I felt.

"Pity we couldn't have stayed longer," I murmured.

"You mean you've enjoyed it enough to want to come back?" Hilary was still smiling... perhaps she understood more than I thought. Then, turning towards the marina, she called out... "Come on kids... time to go!"

I glanced at my watch... nearly noon... we'd be lucky to be home by the children's bedtime. Anna and Michael were hauling on their fishing lines, Anna squealing as a bunch of crabs fell from the hooks and clattered onto the quayside. Nudging with his sandaled feet, Michael persuaded the fearsome-looking crustaceans to scrape and claw their way back to the edge of the precipice.

"Well... that's it for another year," I sighed, climbing into the car. "What's the verdict? Good...? Or was it all a waste of time?"

"It was great, Dad... especially the fishing!" Michael had caught a flatfish off the rocks yesterday; not a bad effort for a ten year old.

I drove slowly, following the narrow road around the curve of the shoreline. Then, gathering speed, we climbed away from the tiny harbour... the Isle of Whithorn. In an hour we'd be off the Machars and heading for Dumfries, then on to Carlisle.

"Shame we couldn't get the TV to work properly," Anna sighed. "I've missed all my favourites."

I glanced at Hilary. "Any special highlights for you?"

"Everything... absolutely fantastic," she said. "Just don't expect any decent meals for the next couple of weeks... I've forgotten how to cook."

I must be positive... I still had a weekend of freedom ahead of me. What about that new CD?

"Some music...!"

"Okay, but not too loud." Anna sounded tired. But then in a more cheerful mood, "I remember this place... this is where we saw the Latinus stone!"

We were entering the town of Whithorn.

I caught a glimpse of the ruined priory, erected in

medieval times on the site of St Ninian's tiny chapel. Recent excavations had uncovered some early Christian crosses, including a roughly inscribed stone which appeared to establish a link with a man named Latinus.

I eased the CD into its slot and the harmonies which emerged were magical; soothing Celtic music with a gentle orchestral accompaniment.

"Goodbye to the Candida Casa." Hilary sounded reflective.

Candida Casa... the ancient name of St Ninian's chapel, now long gone. According to early writers, Ninian had covered its outer walls with a layer of limestone, presumably to make the chapel stand out from a distance. Candida Casa had been interpreted to mean "White House". Could that be the origin of the town's name, I wondered... Whithorn?

At Newton Stewart we joined the coast road and headed east. The Galloway hills soared to our left. To our right the estuary of the Wigtown Bay widened steadily with each mile gained, eventually opening to reveal the full expanse of the Solway Firth.

"How long before we're home?" Anna hated long car journeys.

"Carlisle in a couple of hours," I replied, "and then we're in England."

Inevitably, my mind turned again to thoughts of Monday morning. Staff reports were due at the end of the month. I quite enjoyed writing appraisals for my people, but detested being on the receiving end of them. My boss was tough and uncompromising, recruited not so much for his technical abilities but more because he was supposed to be up to date with the modern approach to business administration and personnel management. I'd made every effort to build a good rapport with him, but without success. So how would he assess my performance? I could only guess. There was no doubt about it; overworked and stressed, I was going through a rough time at the office, and that's what I was heading back towards.

Given the chance, I'd abandon the Home Counties and relocate to Galloway with Hilary. A small cottage... that's all we'd need. But no! I had Anna and Michael to think of, and a house in Surrey to finance.

"How the Celts managed to survive winters up here I can't imagine." Hilary was gazing up at the woodlands rising steeply to our left.

"By staying dry," I replied, "especially when out hunting. A spare set of clothes would have been just as important as a good meal, I reckon."

What this place could do for my archery! There was nowhere to practice down south. Our indoor sports centre was too restrictive. Most of the members were very well-off, with sumptuous properties and second homes abroad. Archery was just another way of flaunting their wealth. All that expensive anti-vibration and counterbalancing gear mounted on high-tech bows had nothing to do with real marksmanship; and with telescopic sights how could they possibly miss the target? Archery was about mastering the longbow. Up here in Galloway I might fine-tune that skill... perhaps end up shooting for Scotland.

Glancing to my right, I saw the broad sweep of the Machars, that wedge of low-lying farmland thrusting its way into the sea. I'd never been here before, but there was something about the scene which stirred my imagination. And the oak-clad hills to my left seemed strangely familiar.

I recalled that faded inscription on the face of the Latinus Stone... the thoughts of an old man... perhaps a dying wish to be reunited with those of his clan who'd gone before him. Maybe Latinus had been a warrior, fated to strut his weary way through a perilous life of mayhem and slaughter. Or a fisherman, destined to take his chances with the tide however rough the Solway Firth.

A signpost flashed by to my left... gone in an instant. But what had it said? Something about Cairn Holy... a Chambered...?

"It's a chambered cairn!" I cried.

Braking hard, I pulled off the road onto a narrow track.

"Oh, Dad...!" Anna protested. "Where are we going now?"

"Richard... no!" cried Hilary. "Where on earth do you think you're taking us?"

"Where are we, Dad?" Michael sounded up-beat... I had an ally.

"We must have missed the turning earlier," I said, "... just one quick look at the cairn."

The track led inland, rising steeply through dense woodland. I began to coax the car upwards.

"For goodness sake, think of the suspension!" Hilary braced herself.

The track was rough, twisting and turning as we climbed in the shadows. I snatched a moment to glance sideways. Amidst the tangle of trees, ferns and jagged rock faces, there were gullies with fast-running streams; torrents of water crashing against boulders topped by layers of luxuriant moss; a paradise for wildlife. Eventually, the canopy became less dense and the full majesty of the forest was revealed in a cascade of sunbeams. A few moments later we rose above the tree line.

"There it is!" Michael yelled.

I stopped the car, and before I could open my door the children were running up a grassy bank towards several tall stones which stood at the top of the mound. Stepping out, I became aware of the vast awning of unbroken sky, above and all around me.

"Look," said Hilary. "Look at the sea... and the Isle of Man." Her mood had changed.

But my eyes were focussed on the cairn; a Celtic grave, like those we'd seen in photographs at the Whithorn museum. As I studied it from a distance, it appeared that the burial chamber had been enclosed by five massive stones, two along each of the longest sides, and one across the narrower western end. Another huge slab had been placed across the top, acting as a ceiling or mantle. To complete the structure, two rough pillars had been raised at the eastern end, acting as flanking stones to mark the entrance of the chamber. The children were kneeling between the flanking stones.

"Dad... there's writing in here!" Anna called.

"You go and see." Hilary moved towards an information plaque. "I'll read this... we might learn something."

I ambled slowly up the bank and crouched beside Anna as she peered into the narrow gap between the flanking stones.

"It's dark inside," she said. "But when your eyes get used to it you can see writing on the stone at the bottom."

She moved aside. And then I began to see them... faint decorations carved on a low-lying flat stone which covered the grave pit. There were spirals; stylised sea creatures perhaps, with long tentacles.

"They must be Celtish drawings," I said. "The Celts were fantastic artists. Nearly everything was curved, just as in nature. They didn't use rulers in those days."

"No Dad... the writing!" urged Anna. "There's writing as well." She was right; there was some kind

13

of script.

"It's a bit difficult to make out," I said. "There might be some Roman letters... the Romans were here two thousand years ago. They probably taught the Celts how to write. That could be a 'G'... and then an 'L'... I can't see the letters in between." I strained my eyes to focus harder. "It could be someone's name, of course... 'Gaelic' maybe...?"

I leaned back and blinked against the bright sunlight.

"Gaelic...?" Michael giggled. "*That's* not a name!"

"Okay... one more time." Again I leaned forward and peered into the gloom. "No, it's not 'Gaelic', but maybe..." I squeezed my eyes and blinked several times. "Maybe it's 'Gaelen'... but I'm still not sure."

"What were the stones for?" Michael asked.

"Thousands of years ago, if you were a very important person, your tribe would bury you here."

"Yuk!" Anna took several steps backwards. "You mean there are skeletons in there?"

"Lots under the mound, I should think. Some might be four thousand years old... perhaps more. But there's only room for one under the stones... probably an old chieftain. He must have been very well thought of to be buried here."

"I wouldn't mind being buried here," said Michael.

Hilary was calling from the foot of the mound.

"There's another cairn further up the hill!"

Then the children were running after her; off to explore the other site.

"I'll stay here!" I shouted after them. "And there's no need to hurry back!"

They were soon disappearing over the brow of the hill. Now I'd have time by myself to fully appreciate the serenity of this sacred place.

I pressed hard against one of the flanking stones

and marvelled at the genius of those early builders. As I looked down, my attention was drawn to a cluster of small brown mushrooms growing at the base of the monument. They looked edible, but I was cautious. Someone had once said there were only two kinds of mushroom hunter... smart ones and dead ones. But surely brown mushrooms were safe. Weren't they eaten raw by the Celts? I plucked one of the smallest, and popped it into my mouth; it melted away and tasted good. I tried another... bigger this time, and then one more.

I listened for birdsong. There was none... perhaps not surprisingly up here well above the tree line. But there was something else; the faintest sound of a harp. I must have left the CD player switched on in the car.

But then I began to feel uneasy... hadn't I removed the ignition key? I fumbled in my pocket, and there it was. And yet the CD player was supposed to be inoperable with the ignition key withdrawn! Confused, I listened intently to the sound. This was different; different to any music I'd heard before. Exquisite, yet delicate and fragile; played on an instrument more primitive than the modern harp.

Once again I found myself reaching out to touch the flanking stone. As my hand moved slowly down its side my fingertips met a small prominence, and beneath it I sensed a tiny niche; then something sharp. With the slightest touch, it fell into my hand... an almost perfectly formed bronze arrowhead!

I shivered, as at that same moment an ice-cold breeze came from nowhere, chilling me to the core. This was no ordinary breath of wind. I'd heard of winters of such savagery that a man might freeze to death in minutes, even under the glare of a midday sun... but at the height of summer?

Still clutching the arrowhead, I moved to the edge

of the mound and scanned the hillside. Below me, the lush blanket of deciduous trees appeared motionless. To my left lay the estuary of the river Fleet... to my right the Machars, and the flat-calm water of Wigtown Bay. Ahead lay the open sea, broken only by the grey contour of the Isle of Man. Yet nowhere was there any trace of that mischievous breeze; it belonged to me alone.

Then, just as swiftly as the cold wind had come upon me, it was gone. Once again I felt the reassuring rays of the sun as it descended over the Machars, moving downwards towards Whithorn some twenty miles to the southwest.

With the arrowhead squeezed tightly in the palm of my hand, I lay on the grass and closed my eyes. It was warmer now, much warmer, and I began to relax. I needed sleep. A short sleep... I was entitled to that, surely.

This was a happy change, and I embraced it. Already, that distant Celtic melody was yielding to a sharper and more penetrating sound. A masterpiece of another order, and of another time, the air around me had begun to resound to the chatter of chaotic bird-song.

CHAPTER 2

I breathed deeply, crouching in the depths of the woodland I knew so well. Advancing slowly I kept low, pausing occasionally to sense the nearness of my target. The undergrowth was thick, but leather sandals and pigskin wraps protected my lower legs. I thought of opening the front of my deerskin jacket to ventilate my upper body; but not now; not at this critical point of the hunt.

The foliage began to thin as I found myself on the edge of a small clearing. And there stood the object of my pursuit. Bathed in the hazy light of a warming sunbeam, and still unaware of my approach, a small deer grazed on the lush grass at the centre of a secluded paradise garden. From this moment, and whatever the outcome, I knew I could feel proud of bringing myself to within such a close range without unsettling this most timid of forest creatures.

I must remain calm and consider the options; to kill, or to reprieve? The deer was small; not much of a problem to carry home. Yet there was ample flesh; enough to provide several meals for my parents and siblings. The hide would furnish a new hunting jacket; the gut a new bowstring.

To kill, then: but with which arrow? Not the barbed variety. Barbs were good for birds and fish, but if this animal were struck with a barbed arrow and not killed

17

quickly it would dash away and suffer an agonising death. I'd use a sharp arrow to strike deep, but one that would withdraw easily should the deer survive the strike.

Down on one knee, my bow at full draw, I held the aim and waited for my arms to steady. The beast raised its head, staring indignantly at me. But the arrow was already gone. The strike was sure, passing through the lower neck and protruding well beyond. The deer tottered for the briefest moment, and was dead before it kissed the grass.

My family would be proud. Tomorrow was the Beltane festival; a celebration of the beginning of summer. There'd be feasting to honour the sun god, Belenus. Hauling the animal onto my shoulders I felt its warmth and caught the musty smell of fungus from its open mouth. I would pace myself: first to cross the tree-clad hills, past the standing stones of my ancestors, then down to the Solway Sea and my father's settlement on the banks of the river Fleet.

At the standing stones, the burial place of our chiefs, I let the carcass fall and took a rest. This was my favourite spot. Seated on the sacred mound high above the tree line I had a spectacular view of the Solway with the Isle of Manannan floating like a giant boat on the horizon.

I'd come here often since that first meeting with Ninian ten summers ago. Ninian was then aged twenty, and I just ten. I was fortunate in that my father had sent me to Novantes to meet the eloquent and personable Ninian. His appetite for knowledge had amazed his teachers, and even the worldly Roman soldiers had been respectful of his abilities, both as a scholar and as an all-round athlete. It was Ninian who'd taught me to think, and it was here at the standing stones that I practised my thinking.

My forefathers were in the otherworld, but their bones were still here, buried deep within this mound. This was their spiritual home, the place where they could meditate upon the fortunes of a territory over which they'd once ruled. I could imagine their spirits, flying like invisible birds into the hearts and minds of the new tribal leaders; those who sought to overcome the afflictions of the present day. One day, my father would be buried here.

Latinus, my father, was good at hiding anxiety... the chieftain must always appear strong. But my mother had told me that he was afraid for his people. Rumours of atrocities in the north had begun to reach our settlement. A race of barbarians, known to our Roman friends as the Picts, was moving steadily south destroying everything in their path.

Suddenly I heard a rustling sound in the under-growth, and then my peace was shattered. From a short distance away came the unmistakable squealing of an enraged boar. And then there was another cry, this time of an animal in distress. I hitched an arrow to my bowstring ready to defend myself and moved forward to investigate.

An uneven fight was under way. Shoulder high above the yellow gorse and lush green bracken, a fully-grown wild boar was running tight circles around a lanky fox-like hound. The hound had been badly mauled and was already in a bad state; its death would be slow and agonising... gored, torn apart, and finally eaten, possibly with its senses reeling and heart still beating. There was no time for refining the aim... I must shoot quickly. The striking power of my bow at close range was immense, and the boar's end was swift.

The hound was male, its coat autumnal brown, almost red in places. Lying on his side and panting furiously, he made no attempt to rise as I approached and knelt beside his lean body. An eye had been gouged from his beautiful head.

My bronze dagger was sharp. It was no sin to send an injured creature to the otherworld. What had our tribal Druid said? "The world of nature is but a gateway to the spiritual realm, where all souls may rest before their rebirth."

I felt for the dagger tucked in my belt. But the hound bedevilled me with his pleading eye... perhaps he wasn't so badly injured after all. He lay still as I probed gently across his bony ribcage, down his thighs and along each of the long spindly legs.

"Complain," I whispered, "and you'll breathe your last." I'd rather kill a badly injured creature than leave it to be scavenged alive.

The hound remained still, and his injuries appeared superficial apart from the loss of that eye.

"You're not ready for the otherworld yet," I murmured. "So what am I to do with you?"

There was movement in his long bushy tail, spasmodic at first, but increasing to a steady rhythm. I knew then I had to carry the animal home; a double load in the sweltering heat.

"But what should I call a one-eyed overgrown fox?" It came to me in a flash. "Balor...!" I exclaimed, causing the hound to flinch.

The tail stopped wagging and I sensed a look of displeasure in that one remaining eye. Balor was the one-eyed sea god... the god of death.

I chuckled quietly to myself; it was hard for me to believe that such gods actually existed. Our tribal Druid had already accused me of blasphemy, criticizing me for listening to the tales of the Roman soldiers. Troopers from the garrison were telling stories about another God... a God who had a son called Jesus who was crucified in a land far away. The Druid had complained to my father that I was abandoning Celtic tradition and opening my mind to these new ideas. And if I was to call my wild, low-born, hound Balor, the Druid would condemn me for being disrespectful. But I didn't care. Although he was our spiritual leader, entrusted by my father with all religious rites, he was also an interfering meddler.

At tomorrow's Beltane festival, our Druid would go into a trance; he'd pretend to reach the otherworld and join with shadowy gods and goddesses. He would claim the spirits had told him about the visitors we could expect in the coming year, about who was to die or be born, and of marriages that were going to take place. But upon recovering from his trance, returning from the otherworld, the Druid would only divulge what was obvious. Most of our people seemed to be taken-in by it... but not me.

I lifted Balor's limp body, tucking him gently under my arm. After just a few paces I stopped dead in my track. In front of me lay the bloody carcasses of his mate and her two pups; the pathetic remains of the family he'd been trying to protect.

I thought about another of our Druid's many sayings... "To meet a wild boar first thing in the morning is bad luck for the rest of the day." For once he was right.

The remaining journey was downhill. Emerging from the woodland, I was spotted by the children of our village. Most of them were still thin and ragged following the privations of the long winter. But they'd soon begin to fill-out and put on weight; rabbits were plentiful again and easily trapped.

"The fox has lost an eye!" cried a young boy.

Short of breath, I felt no obligation to explain, or to point out that it wasn't a fox but a moor hound; a larger version of the same thing. A little girl, running to keep pace with me, reached up and tried to touch the deer.

"Is it dead, Gaelen?"

Her face revealed a trace of sadness. I stopped and bent down to let her stroke its body.

"Not really," I replied. "He still lives among the stars. See if you can find him in the sky... tonight, after the sun has set."

Then an older boy...

"Did the deer die quickly? Can you teach me how to hunt, Gaelen?"

Thoughtful questions... I turned to face the young man.

"Come and see me later. Bring your bow and I'll show you."

Approaching our home at the centre of the village, I saw my mother seated outside. She was drawing a shapeless bundle of wool from her left hand into a long, sleek thread. The fingers of her right hand moved up and down the coil, smoothing the woollen skein, and darting downwards to give extra impetus to a stone which provided the turning action.

Beside her sat Kaylin, my foster sister for the past year. Kaylin was busy assembling small bundles of wool from a much larger batch. Fostering of children with families of other tribes was the custom which pleased me above all others. It often led to marriage, and helped to bond the clans together. Like me, Kaylin was the offspring of a tribal chief. She was in her seventeenth summer and very pretty.

My father, Latinus, sat on the balcony facing my older brother, Ossian. They'd be studying the new board game; a gift from a soldier recently arrived from Rome to join the local garrison. My father was obsessed with board games.

Kaylin glanced up and smiled.

"It's Gaelen!" she cried. "He's finally caught up with his deer!" And then, seeing Balor dangling loosely from under my arm... "But what's that he's managed to find?"

"Latinus!" called my mother, glancing towards the balcony. "Gaelen needs help! Ossian... you too... go and take some of that load from your brother!"

Ossian relieved me of the deer, and father took my bow. A growl from Balor was enough to persuade them that he'd be handled by no-one but me.

"A moor hound will never make a good hunting dog," grumbled father disapprovingly. "And a one-eyed moor hound... it's just another mouth to feed!"

He sounded angry; more than was justified by the mere bringing home of a wild animal. Why was he so hot tempered?

"But the deer was a good catch!" said Ossian, staggering under the weight of the carcass.

Praise from my brother... now that was rare. Ossian was older and much cleverer than me. He could unravel the mysteries of Latin verse, and his knowledge of Roman history, law and custom was immense.

"Kaylin," Ossian went on, "See what a clever little brother I have!" He tottered unsteadily up to her with the deer trailing awkwardly from his narrow shoulders. "It's a shame Gaelen didn't have the brains to complete his studies, though!" He turned and gave me a scornful look. "A pity he has to spend his life tramping across the hills, sweating blood and shooting all the wildlife!"

So that was it... not wishing to be eclipsed by my hunting skills, Ossian was trying to impress Kaylin. And he'd be thinking about tomorrow night's celebrations. Any woman who wanted to conceive would leap the Beltane bonfire with her chosen partner. There was no doubt about whom Kaylin would choose, and it wasn't Ossian. Though gifted in mind, he was awkward and uncoordinated in body. I felt sorry for him. He'd be furious to see Kaylin grasp my hand and lead me off towards the flames of the sun god. And so would my father. I must be careful; father was already angry about Balor.

"Go on, get yourself inside." Mother was ushering me towards the balcony steps. "You must rest."

"A drink for Balor first," I said.

Father drew a sharp breath.

"Balor...?" He mumbled. "A good name is as precious as life. But 'Balor'... it'll bring nothing but death."

Kaylin was already filling a shallow pot with water. Setting Balor down, I watched as he lapped greedily.

"Superstitious nonsense!" cried mother. But I could tell from her face that she disliked the hound's new name. "Latinus," she continued, "why don't you show Gaelen your new board game?"

Leaving Balor to his drink, I climbed the steps behind father. Ossian followed, breathing heavily under the weight of the deer. With a gasp, he dumped the carcass beside the games table.

"I'm getting too old to compete with Ossian," said father, motioning towards the table.

The board was arranged in squares, many of which were occupied by white stones. There were just three black stones remaining.

"The aim," said Ossian, still panting, "Is to immobilise your opponent's stone by placing two of your own on each side of it. Your opponent's stone is then removed... captured!" He drummed on the table beside a pile of black stones, and I began to understand the reason for father's bad temper.

"He's been thrashing me all afternoon," father moaned. "Most of my warriors have been captured. Do you think I've grown too old for war games, Gaelen?"

"Board games aren't important," I replied. "You were a great hunter, father... surely that's what really matters."

"Aye!" he exclaimed, straightening up and grinning broadly... "And I taught you well!" I felt his firm hand on my shoulder as we strolled from the balcony into the cool of the main hall.

As if responding to a silent command our house-slave, Ailsa, entered from the servants' room. Placing a tray of drinking cups on a low table she looked up and smiled at me. Ailsa had nursed me as an infant, often teasing me about my short stature. Compared to Ossian, who'd grown tall and thin, I was still short. But I knew Ailsa was proud of me. She had children of her own, but continued to regard me as a favourite.

"Fresh water, Master...?"

"No, Ailsa... a jug of last summer's wine!" Father waved me towards his favourite chair. "We should celebrate Gaelen's hunting skills!" I felt honoured as he seated himself beside Ossian on a low Roman day bed.

Ailsa brought some elderflower wine from the underground store. It was cool and refreshing.

"Gaelen," said father, "you know that tomorrow is Beltane."

"Yes... and I'm going to prepare the deer for roasting!"

"A fine deer," he laughed. "We should donate it!" Then he added thoughtfully, "Maybe I should offer it to the Druid."

I wished then that I'd left the beast to revel in its earthly pleasures.

25

"You look disappointed," he continued. "You had someone else in mind?"

I remembered the children running to greet me. Many were of the lower social order, hungry and ill clad. Ailsa's own children would have been amongst them.

"We might give it to Ailsa and her family," I suggested.

Father seemed pleased. But then his expression changed... he was growing uneasy.

"Tomorrow... I'll be receiving visitors from the north," he said gloomily. "They'll want to discuss tribal unification, and the Pictish threat."

He glanced at Ossian, and I could tell from Ossian's expression that they'd already discussed the situation.

Perhaps they'd also decided who should attend the meeting. The Druid would have to be there, of course; father would regard his judgement as crucial. And as for me, I was useless at strategy. Was father going to tell me that I'd be excluded from the council assembly?

"The strength of the Roman legionary is diminishing," father continued. "A few are still arriving, but many more are leaving us... there's talk of war in Rome."

"It hasn't always been easy for us to keep the garrison fed," I replied. "Surely things will be easier for us when they leave."

"A typical Gaelen remark...!" exclaimed Ossian. "You just don't see it, do you Gaelen? Just think of the effect on our defensive capability if the Roman's *were* to leave us! Haven't you heard that some of the inland tribal leaders are *already* reporting trouble?" He was about to deliver another of his learned speeches... Ossian always rejoiced in his capacity for logical reasoning. "Tomorrow they'll be telling us..." He stopped short, and I turned to follow his gaze.

Someone else had entered the hall. It was the Druid. He was dressed as usual in a plain white cloak, fastened by a magnificent brooch mounted high on his right shoulder. The twisted gold torc around his neck signalled his high status. His white hair fell straight to his shoulders, and his moustache hung down to blend with a long trailing beard.

"Tomorrow..." said the Druid, as if to continue Ossian's train of thought, "The northerners will be telling us how many sheep and goats they've lost to Pict raiding parties. They will tell us that their villages have been vandalised... that their women have been taken away. They will ask for our assistance... and we must be ready with our answer." Then, as he turned his gaze on me, I saw menace in his penetrating blue eyes. "And yet," he continued, "as Ossian prepares himself for shaping the future of his people, our Chief's *youngest* son seems content to idle away his time in the hills!"

"Not so harsh!" boomed father, springing to my defence. "Gaelen's talents lie in *other* directions. That deer on my balcony... do you think it walked here on its own?" He leaned forward on the day bed, gazing directly into my eyes. "And you've yet to tell me who shall have the deer, Gaelen... have you decided?"

I felt intimidated by the Druid's glare. It would have been easy for me to capitulate to father's earlier judgement, but I wasn't to be discouraged.

"Yes, father... Ailsa's family."

An uncomfortable silence was broken by the sound of footsteps on the balcony. Mother entered, followed by Kaylin.

"Latinus!" exclaimed mother, "a drink for our Druid!" She would never allow visitors to go without some kind of refreshment, especially not a high priest.

Kaylin moved to my side and seated herself on the floor at my feet. The front of her gown fell open slightly, and it was easy for me to see the rise and fall of her lovely breasts. As the daughter of a powerful chief, it was hardly surprising she'd grown into a fine and shapely woman. I wanted to reach out and touch her... to feel her golden hair... but this was neither the time nor the place. She raised her head, our eyes met, and I heard nothing but the sound of her gentle voice.

"You look tired, Gaelen... troubled too. You need to cool down. Why not take a swim... in the sea?"

"Yes..." The sea wasn't my favourite place for swimming... but with Kaylin? "Yes... it's a good day for that. Will you come too?"

She glanced at my mother, perhaps anxious about the spinning still to be done. Mother smiled and nodded. Ossian tried to look unconcerned, but I knew his thoughts. Unable to command a strong physical presence, his major assets were his extensive knowledge and sharp analytical mind. Unfortunately for him, those were not qualities which were stimulating the fair Kaylin... at least not at this present moment.

"And when you've done with your bathing," sneered the Druid, "how will you support your father? How will you summon the warrior god Lugh? How will you persuade Lugh to stand by our Chief when he needs to call upon spear, axe, and swords of bronze and iron to repulse the heathen from the north?"

I was suddenly at the centre of attention. Without much time for thought, my answer was both instinctive and naïve.

"Well..." I swallowed hard. "I've heard talk of a new religion which teaches there's both a heaven and a hell. They say heaven holds fast to those who seek to make peace. But when war begins, then hell opens."

There was another embarrassing silence. Now, more than ever, I realised how unworthy I was to hold the rank of chieftain. I was in my twentieth summer and extremely fit, but a headstrong fool with no stomach for fighting... a disgrace to my father's position. I rose to leave.

"Before you go," said father, "We should tell you of someone who'll be sailing into Novantes over the next few days... a man who left Novantes ten summers ago to sail to France, and then by foot all the way to Rome."

"Ninian...!" I cried, unable to conceal my joy. Ninian was returning after ten long years!

"We've heard he's been made Bishop of Scotland," mother smiled. "...Whatever that means."

"This is becoming a savage place," said father gloomily. "And our people will be poorer without you, Gaelen. But we've long known about that yearning of yours... to carve yourself a meaningful life. Think about it; could this be your opportunity... to revisit Novantes, and to begin shaping your own future?"

"I don't need to think about it... I have to go," I replied.

Father turned to the Druid.

"There, you see... my son will soon be gone," he said. "We must bid farewell to a flame too precious to keep hidden amongst ourselves."

Kaylin took my hand and we moved out into the sunshine.

"Do you see what father has done for me?" I said excitedly.

"He's released you," she replied, her eyes filling with tears. "You're free to leave us." She hesitated for a moment before continuing. "Gaelen... I know you have to go, and I'm happy for you. But when will you return?"

I searched my mind, but could find no answer. We walked in silence down to the shore of the Solway. Then, stripping ourselves to the skin, we ran like children across the sand and into a calm sea. The cold was intense and took my breath away.

"Not too deep!" I cried. I'd seen my younger brother swept off the rocks and drowned many years ago, and feared the sea.

Glancing back towards the beach for reassurance, I saw my new friend, the hound Balor, sitting at the water's edge. He seemed vigilant; watching my every move. Balor, the one-eyed sea god, was on hand to protect me.

Half walking, half floating, I moved steadily towards the now smiling Kaylin. Close enough to feel her breath on my face, I stretched out my arms and felt the firmness of her waist. Closer still, and her breasts were touching mine. Then my arms were around her, and there wasn't a single part of her beautiful body I sensed I couldn't touch.

"I'll leave after Beltane," I whispered. "But I will come back."

As I pressed her to me I gazed over her shoulder, towards the setting sun, and in the direction of Novantes.

CHAPTER 3

Long after sunset a crimson glow continued to illuminate the skyline on the western horizon. I knew this slender light would persist, fading to a dull blue as it moved slowly round to the north... then to the east, brightening steadily to announce the approach of a new dawn. According to our Druid, this was evidence that Belanus, the sun god, never slept in summer, and that a hundred men could slumber in safety under his protection. Belanus would rest only during the long cold nights of winter, when the trees lost their leaves and stood like skeletons against the sky, and when his strength would be reduced to that of ten men.

The huge Beltane bonfire hissed and squealed as the fresh sap-laden wood burst under the tremendous heat. There was a loud crack, and another profusion of sparks rose swiftly from the pyre, swirling in the gentle breeze as they drifted aloft to join the stars.

I reclined on my travelling pack and watched the people of our village resting in their family groups around the great fire, its light reflected in their contented faces. Happiest of all were the children who'd joined hands and were slowly circling the blaze.

We'd endured a hard winter, and our reserves of grain and salted meat had become dangerously low, but life was easier now. The smell of roasting venison hung in the air as one of Ailsa's older children turned the spit. Ailsa had insisted that the whole community should benefit from my kill. The deer was too small to satisfy every appetite, but we also had the wild boar which father had ordered to be retrieved from where I'd left it at the standing stones. Everyone would receive a large slice of wild boar and a tasty piece of venison. Balor, my shy moor hound, lay some distance away. He was gnawing contentedly on one of the boar's enormous shinbones.

I heard the faint sound of music... the Bard of Fleet playing on his tiny harp. He'd be moving from one family group to the next offering poems and songs.

Father sat with the chiefs and some others who'd come from the north to attend his meeting earlier in the day. They'd been discussing battle tactics in the face of the Pictish threat, but were now relaxing, reminiscing and enjoying themselves. Father rose unsteadily to his feet, and approached me carrying an amphora.

"More fire-water for Gaelen...! There'll be precious little of this when you get to Novantes, young hunter!"

"Not too much, Latinus!" cried mother. "The boy has an early start tomorrow; he'll not be fit for the journey."

Kaylin, radiant and beautiful, gazed in silence at the bonfire. She seemed reluctant to meet my eyes. Ossian sat beside her. Sullen and moody, he repeatedly thrust a long stick into the ground.

"And for you, Ossian," said father, "... more wine?" Ossian shook his head vigorously, and said nothing.

"A fine wine, Latinus," said one of the chiefs. "In the past, I could always rely on the commander of our local fort to keep us supplied with good wine. But not now... most of the garrison returned to Rome last winter."

"Ah, but what a send-off we gave them," said one of the escorts. "A warming fire in the great hall, mistletoe for hope, holly for good luck, freshly slaughtered meat... and wine... lots of it, Latinus!"

"It's a miserable thing," said another chief, "that we Britons have contributed so much to the success of the Romans, now only to be abandoned by them."

"Ay!" exclaimed father. "And it's always been the same!"

He slumped back onto his padded cushion.

"I've given *everything* to the Romans," he grumbled. "The best of my fighting men... conscripted into the Roman army! The finest of my warriors... perished in Roman battles! Even as a child... I was assigned a Roman name!"

Then he gazed up into the starry sky, smiling through his pained expression.

"Yet even now," he added, "after all the support we've given them... we are accused of *barbarity* by those we've served so faithfully!"

"Barbarity...?" Ossian leaned forward, frowning.

"Ay... only yesterday!" said father. "A Roman friend tried to persuade me that *my* folk... the fighting Britons of Galloway... the people of my own blood... are accustomed to eating the raw flesh of our enemies!"

Kaylin glanced at father with a mixture of horror and disbelief. He beamed back at her, his face now relaxed... it was all in jest. Though she was the daughter of an important neighbouring chief, Kaylin could still be fooled by one of my father's ludicrous jokes.

Ossian gave another forceful stab with his stick. It snapped, and he reddened with self consciousness. Then, trying to appear unconcerned, he managed to think of something interesting to say.

"One of Ailsa's boys got stung by an adder today."

"No!" exclaimed mother. "Ailsa didn't tell me... when was this?"

"This afternoon... I was passing their hut and saw her youngest son crying. When he told me what had happened I went for the Druid."

"And...?" Mother demanded.

"The Druid came at once... he tore a live chicken in two and put it over the wound." A cruel expression swept across Ossian's face as he continued. "There were feathers everywhere... and lots of blood... all hot and steaming."

Was this Ossian's way of outsmarting father... unsettling Kaylin with an even more shocking tale? I doubted it. His account of the Druid's medication would be accurate. Ossian was very respectful of our Druid... he would never run the risk of creating a scandal by telling a blatant lie.

A look of disgust and loathing had appeared on father's face. I'd often detected a silent rivalry between the Druid and my father. Druid priests were of the highest nobility, and there was little that a chieftain like my father could do to suppress their power. Druids had authority to command sacrifices to appease the gods... it was usually cattle of course, but we'd heard of human blood being offered in some villages.

"The Druid's a forthright man... right enough!" exclaimed father gruffly. He would need to be tactful. Anything said against the Druid was bound to be reported. He turned to reassure my mother. "I'll visit the boy tomorrow morning."

"The Bard of Fleet is coming!" Kaylin had recovered her carefree smile and sounded happy again.

I'd always been fond of the Bard, not simply

because of his amazing skill with words and music, but for his good manners. He'd brought comfort to my mother when my younger brother was drowned. As a child, I once asked him why he'd not become a Druid priest.

"Druids make prophesies," he'd replied, "but only fools listen to them. Besides, I prefer to remain clean shaven."

Tall and upright, I thought he'd have made a fine priest. I'd always turned to the Bard when unhappy during my time at the Roman school. As the son of a chieftain, my teachers had insisted I must study the glories and savageries of the past to fully appreciate my place in the world. But I hated their lessons... I would rather spend my time in the forest with the animals.

"But its *right* that you should learn about these things," the Bard had encouraged, "... for it's better to be unborn than untaught. Study hard, Gaelen... while you are still young. When the twig is tender it's easier to bend, just like your bow."

Fortunately for me, the Bard had plenty of insight; more than my teachers. Wasn't it he who'd suggested to father that I might benefit from a short stay at Novantes in the company of Ninian?

The Bard seated himself in front of Kaylin and studied her face for a while.

"There is much sadness at the parting of our young hunter," he said softly. "What can we say... perhaps to make him change his mind?"

The fingers of his right hand were already down upon the strings of the tiny harp, and a tremulous sound emerged. Having first established a rhythm, he softened the volume a little, and began his poem:

For the young hunter who will travel tomorrow,
A cloak made from wool we shall weave.
But for that he must wait beyond cockcrow...
For the sheep's on the hill... and won't leave!

There was a ripple of laughter from the crowd which had begun to gather around us.

Ay, the wool's on the sheep in the wasteland
And the loom's in a tree... on the hill.
The shuttle...? It's with the King of all Ireland
And the bobbin...? It's now lost in the mill.

Then, turning to me,

And the hunter... who would leave us so swiftly...
Abandoned to our grief and disorder?
His cloak... it will appear so unsightly...
For our weaver's not yet born to her mother.

What was he saying? That I would never receive my cloak of wool? That I must remain here, never to venture away from my own people? Surely, the Bard knew me better than that.

He'd stopped playing, and there was silence; save for the crackling of the great fire and a monotonous grinding as the remains of the deer and wild boar were turned on their spits. Kaylin's cheeks glistened with tears.

Then I heard whispering... I looked up and saw the Druid approaching. The atmosphere grew tense and expressions of calm turned to apprehension as he strode into our midst and settled himself beside my parents, his head and shoulders elevated above my father's.

A small boy was the first who dared speak.

"Gaelen... you promised to show me how to hunt

for deer."

"And so I did!" I saw a look of disappointment on his face. "But I can't... not now... not for a while." I glanced towards father. "Chief Latinus will string a bow and teach you how to shoot, won't you father?"

"The deer is a very *special* creature!" the Druid interrupted. "A gentle goddess was once compelled by an evil wizard to take the form of a deer."

I knew the Druid would spoil our evening by trying to dominate the conversation, boring everyone with his fairy tales, but I felt powerless to prevent it.

"The goddess," he continued, "was allowed to show herself as a woman only to a certain young man named Finn. She became Finn's mistress, but was forced to change back into a deer whenever Finn was away from her."

I glanced towards the Bard. He sat with his head lowered.

"One day," droned the Druid, "Finn entered the forest to look for his goddess, but found instead a small naked boy. Finn recognised the boy as his own son by the goddess, and called his son Ossian. Ossian grew to become a great poet and musician... the best ever!" Then, looking at our Bard, he added, "...Which is something our present company would do well to remember!"

Another myth... and a compliment to my brother's knowledge of literature... but the effect on our Bard! This was an attack on his artistic accomplishments, and he would feel badly maligned. The Druid and the Bard never seemed to enjoy each others' company.

As the Bard raised his head he must have seen the Druid grinning back at him contemptuously.

"And as for those of us who *do not* believe in such idle rubbish," said the Bard calmly, "it's as well that our teeth are in front of our tongues."

He sounded unruffled, but I knew how he must be feeling.

"Take heed, Druid!" the Bard continued. "Harmless fairy-tales are one thing, but a morbid fascination with make-believe is the sign of an inferior mind!"

The Druid's eyes widened, his face reddening and mouth gaping.

We were on the brink of a feud. I had to say something... offer support to the Bard. But I felt outclassed and ill-equipped for intellectual argument. I would choose another way... try to restore harmony.

"So...," I said, turning to the boy. "Before you draw your arrow against a deer, be sure you're well trained. Finn's goddess will be angry if you can't achieve a clean kill."

"Talk to us about the water spirits, Druid!" Ossian called out. His face bore the look of flattery. "The *evil* spirits... the ones you tried to frighten us with when we were young."

Was this Ossian's way of calming a difficult situation... to invite yet *another* lesson in Celtic myth? Surely the children had become weary of water kelpie stories. It was more likely that Ossian was ingratiating himself with the Druid... trying to gain favour.

"Speaking for myself," I said, trying to lighten the conversation, "I've never been scared of water spirits. But I've always been afraid of the sea... ever since the day my younger brother was drowned whilst we were fishing off the rocks."

I felt a cold shiver down my spine as the Druid darted a disapproving look in my direction. Then he stood up, raising his hands and eyes to the stars.

"It is not the power of the sea you fear!" he cried, "but the wrath of Manannan! Ay, Manannan... the champion of gallant sailors! Manannan never harmed a *brave* fisherman!" he roared. "Riding upon his horse, Splendid Mane, Manannan caresses the waves seeking mariners in distress... his boat, Wave Sweeper, forever ready to carry a drowning man to the safety of the otherworld!"

"Ay!" chorused the village folk, their sparkling eyes rolling upwards to follow his demented gaze.

Ay, I thought... but Manannan wasn't on the scene when I saw my younger brother being dashed help-lessly against the rocks. It pained my heart to recall his choking cries for help, the blood pouring from his lacerated hands as they clawed at the barnacles, and then his limp body, face down as it floated away on the billowing waves. There was no sign then of a horse called Splendid Mane, or of any boat named Wave Sweeper.

But there was no stopping our Druid now; he was remorseless. Fired with passion, there followed praises to Danu, the universal goddess whose husband was Bile; tributes to Dagda, the good god who ate porridge and gave food to everyone in proportion to their merits; a devotion to Aine, the goddess of love, and daughter of the son of Manannan. When announcing that Aine had slain King Olom with her magic as he tried to rape her, the Druid became ecstatic.

And then he fell silent... breathless. Casting his eyes downwards, first towards Ossian and then to Kaylin, he grasped their hands and pulled them both to their feet.

"The fire of Belanus still burns!" he yelled, turning them around to face the bonfire. "The time has come to bond young hearts in sacred marriage. Tonight, Belanus will unite Ossian and Kaylin... the unification of two tribes by the conjunction of their chieftains' offspring!"

I could hardly believe it! My parents hadn't spoken

of this. Kaylin's own family hadn't been consulted; at least not to my knowledge. Father looked dumbfounded. I glanced at mother; she appeared traumatized. By now, several other couples were racing towards the flames. Ossian looked nervously at Kaylin, eager for her to join him, but hesitant.

"Forward, my child!" the Druid howled at Kaylin. "Embrace the flames... give pleasure to the sun god Belanus; celebrate his spouse, the Moon; bring honour to Venus, his page.... let Belanus plant the seed of Ossian within you!"

Ossian's seed...? Inside Kaylin...? I leapt to my feet. Passing the bowstring over my head, I secured the bow across my shoulder and fastened the quiver around my waist. Then I took hold of my bed pack. Of course Ossian must become the leader of our people on the death of my father. Of course he would find in Kaylin the perfect partner. I was nothing. My thoughts were always for the natural world. I'd always been left out of important meetings. Unlike Ossian, I'd never been confined by ritual grooming for high command. Ossian had studied the written word, Roman law and religion. I was a hunter, that's all... a wild man... an idle dreamer. I wasn't worthy of Kaylin. I would leave tonight. I'd go now, and try to forget my misery... the anguish and the jealousy.

Cries of joy mingled with yelps of pain drifted from the bonfire as others began to leap the flames. And yet, despite the Druids prompting, Kaylin remained immoveable. She turned and took a step towards me, and then another with her hand outstretched. She was grasping my free hand, pulling me towards the fire. I resisted. Moments ago I'd set my mind on a quiet, ignominious departure. The transformation was unreal; too sudden. But I felt myself giving way. With Kaylin's hand in my right hand, and clutching the bed pack in my left, I found myself sprinting towards the blaze; over the lush grass; across a stretch of ground charred black by the heat; through the white ash which marked the outer edge of the fire; and into the intense heat still radiating from its glowing embers. To stumble now would have spelled disaster.

Ahead, at waist height, the angry flames beckoned. It was difficult to coordinate the jump, but somehow we sailed through. Kaylin landed short and fell. As I hauled her from the smoking cinders, she was laughing. We embraced, and I tasted her mouth; sucking the perspiration and flecks of charcoal from her cheeks and neck; breathing the fragrance of her golden hair.

There might have been more, so much more... but not now. Kaylin had shown to everyone that I was her man. She knew I must travel alone to find a purpose for my life, and that I would eventually return to my father's village on the banks of the Fleet. As I pulled back, she reached between her breasts and withdrew a small tawny coloured object.

"It's a Bride doll, Gaelen," she said.

She offered it, and I felt its smoothness; the doll had been beautifully crafted.

"I made her from last years straw... keep her with you. Lay her in your bed before you sleep... and bring her safely home."

Tears mingled with soot ran in streaks down Kaylin's face, but even now she was managing to smile.

I backed slowly away, separating myself from the heat, the glow of the fire, and becoming absorbed into the night as I moved towards the darkened forest behind me. She watched as the gap between us widened. I was saying goodbye in my heart... to Kaylin, to my family, to my friends, to my birthplace, and to my past. I took a deep breath and turned to face the west.

Ahead, enveloped by the darkness, stood the Galloway hills; broad and massive, bathed in the meagre light of the stars. My destination lay somewhere beyond those hills, in a land known as the Machars. Low on the skyline to my right, faint traces of blue betrayed the presence of daylight in other lands as the midnight sun passed well below the northern horizon.

I would stride briskly uphill to the standing stones, say farewell to the spirits of my forefathers, then move onwards; towards Novantes and my new life.

CHAPTER 4

Would I find my way to Novantes? Would Ninian remember me, the child who once came to stay? Would he have regard for the grown man, a simple hunter? These were the questions which preyed on my mind.

I needn't have worried about losing my direction; little had changed since I'd travelled this way ten summers ago.

Yesterday I'd come down from the hills. Passing through thick forests, I'd paused to rest alongside cascading torrents of cool water, feasting on the fern-like leaf of the chervil, root of the dandelion, leaves of the plantain and coltsfoot. I was heading south now, and making good progress through the gently rolling countryside of the Machars.

Over to my left I could see the Solway, and the steadily widening bay which separated me from my home on the banks of the Fleet. Having spent the first night walking, and a further two nights sleeping under the stars, I was now into my third day of travel; lacking for nothing except company.

And yet, I was being watched. I'd known it from the start; just as a wild animal knows when it's being stalked by an incompetent hunter. My suspicions had been confirmed early this morning. Whilst rolling my bed pack into a tight bundle I'd noticed something close to where my head had lain; the partially gnawed shin bone of a wild boar. There was no doubting who was responsible. Balor was on the prowl, following in my footsteps... perhaps anxious that I shouldn't starve. Before his encounter with the boar, Balor had reigned as a supreme hunter: a master of stealth. Now, hampered by the loss of an eye, his instinctive stalking abilities would have been seriously impaired; until last night, that is, when he'd crept to my side as I slept. I placed the bone in my travelling pack and wondered when he might decide to show himself.

The sun blazed down, and although I was extremely fit I began to feel footsore and weary. Suddenly, my attention was captured by a flash of reflected sunlight from the summit of a low lying hill. At long last, I must be approaching Novantes. That glint of light may have been the gleam of polished armour... wasn't there a Roman camp at Rispain, a mile or two beyond the village?

I trudged on, and eventually arrived at the boundary of Novantes. Passing through an opening in the earthen embankment, I began to recognize some of the old dwellings I'd seen as a child. But the settlement was deserted... except for a few skinny dogs which lay panting in the sweltering heat, and some scrawny chickens scratching and pecking in the dry earth.

I looked for the home of Ninian's parents. Like me, Ninian was the son of a chieftain so his family would occupy the largest building. It would have a balcony from which the chief could oversee the other dwellings and address his people.

Ninian had set out for Rome ten summers ago, at the peak of his physical powers. Now aged thirty, would he still be as good at competitive sports? Would he still know me?

The chieftain's home was on higher ground at the centre of the village, just as I'd remembered. But it seemed abandoned. Climbing the balcony steps to gain a better view, I began to feel alarmed as the uncanny silence took hold of me. Had the settlement been attacked? It seemed unlikely. Situated in a shallow valley, Novantes was well concealed from raiders approaching from the sea... much less vulnerable than my father's settlement at Fleet. I scanned the village for signs of destruction, but there were none.

I felt unwelcome... rejected. To have come so far and to be offered nothing but silence was a sign; an angry gesture from the gods. Our Druid had been right to chastise me for blasphemy, and to humiliate me in front of my family. It was no more than I deserved. I'd failed to demonstrate respect for the war god Lugh, and now the spirits of the otherworld were clawing back at me. But I'd only recently become sceptical... largely due to the Bard's influence. Although the Bard was a good man, he was partly to blame for my wayward views. As a child I'd been enraptured by tales of the otherworld; perhaps if I was to focus my mind and summon up those legends again, then maybe... just maybe... the gods would be lenient with me.

I recalled the tale of Lugh's spear; the javelin which had a life of its own, which thirsted for blood, and whose blade had to be kept in a bed of crushed poppies to keep it calm between battles. I struggled to remember its other powers; its strength to alter the flight of its opponent's spears, and to blunt the swords of its enemies. But my faith in Lugh was too tenuous... I couldn't bring myself to dwell on fairytales. Our Druid knew the truth; I was useless to the gods and to mankind... the second rate son of a chieftain, with no stomach for battle and no aptitude for leadership.

From my elevated position I saw the lazy dogs beginning to rise sluggishly and creep away on their spindly legs. The chickens too were leaving the scene. I was being abandoned. Hardly surprisingly, I thought; you can't bring luck to a luckless man, and bad luck is as contagious as scabies.

As I looked down, a large red moor hound sauntered across the open space in front of me. Balor! So *that's* why the other animals had turn-tailed. There was no disputing the authority of Balor amongst these domesticated creatures. He loped casually up to a small dwelling, sat down beside it, and stared at me with that one remaining eye. But why had he chosen this moment to reveal himself? As I watched, a faint wisp of smoke rose from the roof of the dwelling; it must be occupied! The smell of cooking had drawn him in!

I bounded down the balcony steps and strode purposely forward. Balor moved nimbly away.

Like most Galloway buildings the hut was circular, with a wall of interlaced twigs and mud. The roof was of straw and turf, with a vent to allow the free escape of smoke. But smoke will go where it pleases, and some of it was finding its way through fissures in the wall. Bending down to peer inside the low entrance I heard a faint metallic sound, like the clank of an iron pot.

"Anyone there...?" I called.

There was a gasp, then silence.

"I've travelled many miles to see a friend." Still silence.

After what seemed a long time, I heard a shuffling sound. Then, a tiny old woman peered out from the shadows covering the lower part of her face with a rough shawl.

"I'm alone," I said, stepping back. "And I'm sorry

if I frightened you."

Her old eyes moved slowly, taking in my tousled hair, my deerskin jacket, the bow slung over one shoulder, my travelling pack over the other; then downwards to my short trousers, and finally to my leather sandals, well worn and very dusty. She must see that I was no painted warrior; no Pict. She let the shawl drop from her face and lowered her scrawny arm to her side.

"Who are you, and where do you come from?" she croaked.

What remained of her teeth were a dreadful mess, but there was a kindness in that worn and weary expression.

"My home is by the river Fleet. My father..." I paused. Yes of course my father was the leader of his tribe and a prominent ally of the Romans; but what of it? "My father... has allowed me to visit Novantes, so that I may see a friend, Ninian."

Her thin lips began to tremble. She frowned, and then her mouth broke into a craggy smile.

"Ah," she said. "The young Gaelen... you'll be the young Gaelen. But see how you've grown!"

She stretched out her arms towards me, drawing me into her smoky home. Seated on a stool beside the central fire, a large bowl of water appeared at my feet. With my aching ankles comfortably immersed, she placed a bowl of steaming soup on my lap. If the otherworld exists, I thought, it must surely be here at Novantes. Raising the bowl to my mouth, I gulped down the nourishing liquid. It was game soup; my favourite.

"You don't recognize me, Gaelen? I'm Curzen... house slave to Ninian's parents." She sat opposite me, taking my wet feet onto her lap and drying them with a soft woollen towel. "I see all who come and go. I remember how you came to stay many summers ago... how you loved to play ball with the other children. And I remember how you tried to outplay the young Ninian, but he was too old for you... too big, too fast." Then, with a wistful look, "Ay, he'd be ten years your senior; then as now."

The past came flooding back. Ninian had been a supreme athlete. He'd spoken Latin fluently, and was much inspired by tales of sporting events described by the Roman soldiers.

"He told me about games which are played every four summers in another land," I said. "And about men who train hard and who expect handsome rewards for their running, long jumping, discus, javelin and wrestling."

"Ay," she replied with a glint in her eyes, "and did he tell you those athletes perform naked?"

Naked athletes...? I racked my brains for a credible explanation.

"Well... I've heard it's very warm in other lands."

"Nay!" she cried. "They used to be clothed, right enough, but then one competitor accidentally lost his waist tunic and they've been naked ever since! And see here... they're *big* men, Gaelen. Did you not hear of the athlete who won the grand prize in five successive games?"

I shook my head. Revelations like these were not common in my village. But Novantes had a sea port; frequent visitors from overseas would keep the people here well informed.

"Why," she continued, "on the last occasion he carried the sacrificial ox right around the stadium on his shoulders; and then sat down and ate the whole thing!"

An interesting story, maybe, I thought... but not important... not right now.

"And when is Ninian expected to return?"

"When...?" she exclaimed. "But he's arrived! His ship has been seen... all the people are down at the harbour to greet him!"

Lifting my feet off her lap, she rose briskly and beckoned me to follow.

I slipped into my sandals, now hard and abrasive against my tender ankles, and hobbled behind Curzen out into the sunshine. I remembered the harbour was a long way off.

"From that hilltop..." she said, pointing towards the south, "you'll see the Solway. It's a short walk from there to the harbour... the Isle of Novantes... that's where you'll find them."

A well trodden path made the going easy, but it seemed like an age before I reached the brow of the hill. Breathing vigorously, I glanced back and saw Novantes in its entirety; a flimsy assemblage of huts nestling within an earthen boundary... and the solitary figure of Curzen still gazing after me with her arm held aloft. I waved back, and then faced the way ahead.

The sparkling sea was coming into view, and I could just make out a wooden jetty and some fishing huts lining the edge of an almost circular harbour.

But it was none of those things which held my attention. The tide was full, and I stood awestruck by the sight of a magnificent ship lying at anchor in the middle of the bay. This was no fishing boat, no inshore trading vessel. It must be an ocean going ship. I'd seen such craft from my vantage point at the standing stones high above Fleet, but only from a great distance. I couldn't have imagined they were so long in the keel, so wide in the beam, or carry so much sail, now neatly furled under the yardarm.

I hurried on, and eventually moved down onto the

49

pebbled beach where I was confronted by a scene of lively activity. Coracles were plying their way to and from the ship, offloading men and cargo. A few Roman soldiers were being rowed ashore, but many more were lined up on the beach as if waiting to board. Local men were bending themselves to the task of hauling wooden boxes, crates, amphorae and bundles of rope up from the shoreline, whilst women and children lingered in groups watching from a distance.

One young mother stood apart from the others, tall and elegant, with long black hair falling to her waist. A small boy and a slightly older girl were hiding behind the skirt of her long grey dress. I moved closer.

"They work hard," I said. "Like honey bees... but I prefer to watch."

She glanced at me briefly, and then turned back to face the ship. It had been a stupid thing for me to say, and I suddenly felt awkward.

"I mean, I wouldn't... I couldn't... be of any help. It's my first visit to a major anchorage, you see. It's so muddled... confusing. Where did it come from... the ship? Do you know?"

Now she was studying me closely, and I her. Her face was thin and pale. There was a gracefulness about her... beauty even.

"It's always this way when a ship arrives," she said. "Everyone comes to help... that one's from France."

"From France...!" I tried to grapple with a geography I hardly knew. If only I'd kept to my studies instead of squandering my youth, perfecting my skill as a marksman and hunter. "I don't... I don't understand," I stammered. "Soldiers come from Rome... surely this ship is from Rome."

"Well yes," she replied, "we have ships from Rome

sometimes, but more often they come from France... and England, Wales, Ireland... you're not from Novantes, I think."

"No," I sighed. "Not from here..." I felt cheated, and allowed the sound of my voice to fade away. I'd been misled by the human race, and outwitted by the gods; Ninian wasn't coming back after all.

"From where, then...?"

I didn't answer straight away. My attention had been drawn to a small group of men disembarking from one of the larger coracles. They were simply attired, not in traditional animal hide, but in long grey gowns. As they lowered themselves into the water to take the last few steps to the shoreline I noticed they were barefoot. They moved carefully over the stones, lifting their gowns to avoid a soaking, their greyness, simplicity and total lack of ornamentation setting them apart from the crowd.

"I'm from a village by the river Fleet." As I spoke my attention remained fixed on that band of men. "I came to see an old friend... Ninian."

One of the men tripped and fell headlong into the water. His companions were laughing as he staggered to his feet and stumbled again. I turned to the woman; she was smiling at me.

"Ninian's my brother," she said. "He came ashore a little while ago. Those men..." she nodded towards the small group, now gingerly making their way up the stony slope, "they're his assistants." Then she pointed towards another group. "And there are our parents."

The chief of Novantes, accompanied by his wife, stood with several other people, including a Roman commander dressed in a uniform emblazoned with magnificent feathers and shining medallions. My senses reeled from this sudden turn of events.

"But... but Ninian isn't with them!"

"No," she sighed. "It seems my brother's too proud to be seen with his own family. I don't know where he is now... but not far away, I'm sure."

Bidding farewell to Ninian's sister, I moved towards his colleagues, now resting on a grass bank well above the waterline. There were five of them, all clearly exhausted. One, a short stout man, looked up as I approached.

"Wake up, Brothers!" he exclaimed. "Here comes a brave young warrior from Galloway!" I didn't recognize his accent, and found myself struggling to understand what he was saying. "Greetings, champion," he continued. "My name is Fabian." He outstretched his arms and bowed his head. "We are at your service!"

The group seemed amused as I became the centre of attention.

"You must forgive our little outburst," said the man next to Fabian. "But you can't imagine what a relief it is to be back on dry land."

This man's accent was more familiar. He looked very pale... almost green.

"The sea is calm in the bay," he added, "but exceedingly wrinkled beyond the horizon. My name is Stephen."

"And mine Gaelen," I replied. "I'm a friend of Ninian."

There was a long silence as they exchanged glances.

"Why yes, young Gaelen," said a third, reaching down to the pebbled beach with his bare feet. "But you'll not find Ninian here."

This was the man who'd suffered an untimely swim in the shallows. He was older than the others; tall, slender, almost completely bald, and still dripping.

"I'm Brother John." He stepped closer. "If you

wish to see Bishop Ninian, you'll find him in a small cove... just over that rise." He was pointing to an out-crop of land away to the north. "Ninian was most anxious to be alone; to be re-acquainted with the land of his birth."

"Thank you... I'll go now." I felt self-conscious and out of place in their company.

"Have a care, young Gaelen," warned Fabian. "We Brothers are all given to silent contemplation, but solitude is food and drink to Bishop Ninian."

"Especially at this time," added John.

With mixed feelings I turned and headed north, keeping close to the edge of the bay and leaving the ship behind. Then I climbed over a narrow strip of land which separated the anchorage from the smaller cove which lay ahead. This must be the 'Isle' of Novantes... a small protruding headland that was once a real island.

It would soon be evening. I felt the sun on my back as I stood on the edge of the tiny cove, its mouth opening to the Solway Sea and facing my home in the Galloway hills, still clearly visible on the distant horizon.

My shadow lay ahead of me, extending out beyond the pebble beach and over the smooth water. I was mesmerised, partly by the illusion of this sudden rise in my physical stature, but also by the silence.

Then, along the right hand side of the bay which was still bathed in sunlight, I saw the grey-clad figure of a man seated on a rock, bent forward as if deep in thought.

Like an excited child I scrambled down the rocky bank. Half running, half stumbling over the rounded pebbles, I panted my way towards Ninian. Surely he must have seen me by now... the clatter of stones under my feet must have distracted him!

A few paces from my old friend, I came to a halt. But Ninian was still leaning forward, resting his chin in both his hands. This was not the image I'd expected; not the robust and carefree young athlete I remembered from ten summers ago. Was this the 'quiet contemplation' that Fabian had mentioned? Ninian seemed to be weighing all the troubles of the world.

Then, very slowly, he turned to me, his face thin and pale. But there could be no mistaking those blue eyes still shining with an intensity which communicated a true friendship. Here, I knew, was a man with the kindliness to listen, and the capacity to understand.

At first there was nothing but silence between us. But then he rose to his feet and held out his arms.

"Gaelen," he smiled. "The young hunter from Fleet has come to welcome a little fish from the sea."

I stumbled forward and fell into the embrace of my tall, lean, and godlike friend.

CHAPTER 5

Curzen had given over her tiny hut to Ninian and his Brothers so they wouldn't have to sleep out in the open. They'd protested vigorously, of course, emphasising that the nights were warm and dry and that they were young and made of sturdy stuff. They'd demanded to know where Curzen herself would sleep. It was explained she'd be staying at the chieftain's house over the next few days, serving as a cook and waitress while Ninian's parents entertained a Roman centurion newly arrived on the ship with Ninian's group earlier in the day.

As we sat around the fire, I watched our shadows flickering around the circular wall. The sun had set a long time ago, and I felt drained, emotionally and physically; almost lulled to sleep by the low, continuous murmur of my companions' voices, talking in a strange language I didn't know. But they'd travelled so much further than I had, and on the high seas in great danger. Surely the least I could do was to wait until they'd retired to bed... but for how long? I ached for sleep. Was it possible these stalwarts of the Christ God didn't need their sleep? The stout little Fabian seemed to notice my predicament, and turned to me.

"You are not hearing what we say?" he asked. Now he was speaking my language again, but still with that strange accent.

"I haven't understood a word," I replied. "But I always find things difficult before they become easy... it's taken me all my life to learn to shoot a fast-moving rabbit and kill it cleanly with a single arrow."

It was some consolation to me that I could do that, even though I couldn't enter their conversation.

"You must come to live in my country, Gaelen," Fabian continued, "... not to shoot with rabbits, but to understand my language, the customs and artistic achievements of France... yes?"

"Let him be, Fabian!" exclaimed John. "And don't be fooled, Gaelen... France is under attack by savages. Imagine going out hunting, only to be confronted by hordes of marauding barbarians."

He leaned forward to push some unburned wood towards the centre of the fire.

"Setting up a steady aim is one thing," John continued, "but try aiming from a *moving* platform. Those monsters... they shoot with extreme accuracy from the backs of galloping horses!" He turned to face me. "Besides, if you lived in France you wouldn't have a midnight sun to guide your nocturnal hunting, would you?"

"That's true," said Stephen. "Beware of Brother Fabian, Gaelen; he'll have you transported across the sea to France before sunrise. I don't know how we persuaded him to leave."

"I still don't understand," I said, turning to Ninian, "I thought you'd come from Rome."

"I left Rome last summer," Ninian smiled. "But I stopped for a while at Bishop Martin's monastery in France. I was joined there by these Brothers of mine... the best missionaries I could have wished for. John and Stephen are priests, Gaelen. They'll spread the news of God to every corner of Galloway. Fabian is our scribe. He'll produce written words... teach people to read, and encourage them to learn about Jesus Christ. Marcus and Felix are builders... and build we must. There has to be a *centre* of worship... a place of sanctuary where people can find God."

I'd yet to meet with Marcus and Felix. There hadn't been room for them in Curzen's hut, so they'd been accommodated in another part of the village.

"Aren't there already lots of good buildings in Novantes?" I said. "Couldn't you use one of those as a sanctuary?"

Ninian turned and nodded towards John, as if inviting him to enlighten me.

"Ninian has a *stone* building in mind," John explained. "...A stone chapel. Rome began as a tiny settlement, Gaelen, just like Novantes and your own village at Fleet. But Rome grew bigger... much bigger, with temples, roads, bridges and public works all built of stone... of stone, Gaelen... not of wood, mud and turf."

"I spent a year in Rome, finishing my training," added Stephen. "You should see their warm baths, Gaelen. They've every facility for bathing. But the baths are also a place where people meet, with libraries, picture galleries and lecture halls."

They were overestimating the depth of my knowledge and understanding. I'd never seen a stone building, and although I could well appreciate the pleasures of a warm bath, what could I be expected to know of those other things?

"A far cry from what we have here in Novantes," said Ninian. "And yet our lives can be frittered away by too much detail... we must strive for simplicity, whilst continuing to build on the work done by Bishop Martin."

"You've mentioned him before," I said.

"Bishop Martin was a Roman soldier," explained Stephen. "But he saw the light and became a pacifist. He was imprisoned and treated very badly, but rose above the opposition and trained as a priest. He was eventually made a Bishop, and assigned to work in France. He's dead now, but his example will never die."

"And he lived most of his life in France!" claimed Fabian proudly.

"But he was no Frenchman," added John. "He was half Roman, half German." And then with a grin, "...But yes, he did *live* like a Frenchman... they say he was a very untidy man, with unwashed clothes and tousled hair!"

John and Stephen burst out laughing, while Ninian remained placid and Fabian looked resentful.

"God is rarely to be found amongst fine clothes and well-groomed hair," interrupted Ninian, "... and there's many a splendid cloak which hides a wretched spirit." Then he turned to me. "What made Bishop Martin special, Gaelen, is that he went out from his monastery to spread the word of God... to convert the barbarians, and to encourage a greater knowledge of agriculture, carpentry and working in metals. It's an example which we are determined to follow."

Suddenly, there was movement at the entrance. A woman appeared. The fire had died to a steady glow, but there was still enough light for me to see that it was Ninian's sister whom I'd met at the harbour. I felt a surge of excitement.

"So this is where my brother chooses to hide on his first day home," she smiled. "Our festivities are at an end Ninian... it's safe for you to return to your family."

"But this is a pleasant enough retreat, Apolonia," replied Ninian. "And you haven't yet been introduced

58

to John and Stephen, my priests... or to Fabian, my talented scribe."

Remaining seated, they bowed their heads towards Apolonia. Then Ninian turned to me, pausing for a moment as he scanned my face.

"And this is my friend, Gaelen," he said. "But you've already met, I think."

How could he have known about my earlier meeting with Apolonia? Had she told him, or had he read my thoughts?

Apolonia smiled again, and I felt strongly attracted to her. My heart beat faster as our eyes met.

"You managed to find my itinerant brother, Gaelen. I hope you're not tempted to join him as he wanders like a dreamer across the world."

I was tongue-tied, and Apolonia turned again to Ninian.

"Your friends are speechless with exhaustion," she said. "They've been invited to sleep here. Curzen will lodge with us. As for you... you must do as you please, Ninian."

"I'll come now," he replied. "I must speak with father."

Ninian rose to follow Apolonia out of the hut, leaving me with his three Brothers to prepare our beds.

"My body feels as if it is being tossed by the waves," murmured Fabian as he unrolled his bed pack. "I am still riding the storm... but I feel so tired that I would be content to sleep with the Picts and the Visigoths tonight."

I'd heard about Picts... but Visigoths? I hadn't the energy to enquire.

My last thought was for Balor. He'd trailed me all day, and I knew he would be close by. Taking his bone from my travelling pack, I stooped low and moved outside into the cool night air. He'd generously donated the bone to me. The marrow would still be edible, but I'd dined well this evening and it was right that Balor should have it back. I placed his bone in some long grass and returned to the hut.

"An offering to your Celtic gods?" enquired John.

"To a living Celtic god," I replied. Then, with my head laid on my travelling pack, I was quickly ensnared by the power of sleep.

*****

Waking to the sound of a barking dog, I lay still for a moment, waiting for my eyes to focus and trying to remember where I was. It seemed only moments ago I'd slipped into unconsciousness. Surely it couldn't be morning already? In the dim light I saw the remnants of ash from a fire, three small bundles of personal belongings, a circular wall of mud and thatch, and a roof of turf.

My three companions had gone! The Brothers had deserved their rest, yet they'd risen early whilst I'd been content to laze away the morning... succumbing to sloth. I was soon on my feet and moving out into the brilliant light of a new day.

Standing at the entrance, I took in the sights and sounds of a bustling community of Novantes folk. A woman stood in a small enclosure tossing corn to the domestic fowl. An old man, deformed with a hump back, tried to serve a bucket of swill to three ferocious wild boars loosely tethered to a wooden stump. He was trying to keep a safe distance, hobbling first to the left and then to the right, intent on finding a lucky opportunity to penetrate their feeding area. The poor man cursed and spat as the beasts lunged at him.

I looked for Balor's bone... it had disappeared.

Heading for the village pond, I removed my deer-skin jacket and knelt to wash, sweeping the cool water over my arms and upper body. Then I leaned forward, immersing the whole of my face for as long as I could hold my breath. Drawing back with a gasp, I began to feel refreshed and alive again.

Two pretty young women had arrived with some clothes to wash. Kneeling at the edge, they stared at me. Then, turning to each other, they began to giggle. Soon, they were hopelessly convulsed. I felt shy and embarrassed. No-one had ever laughed at my bare chest before... Kaylin had never scorned my body... she'd always been stimulated by my nakedness. Then I was startled by the shrill sound of a woman's voice from behind...

"Hold your silly tongues! Have you no work to do?"

I spun round... it was Curzen. One short scolding from the old lady was enough to end the drama. But then her craggy features began to melt.... her mouth opened, giving vent to unconstrained laughter.

"It's your hair Gaelen!" she wheezed. Reaching up, I felt my long hair pointing upwards and outwards in all directions. Unwashed and greasy, it was transfixed in disarray after its drenching. "Come with me," she beckoned.

Back at her hut she washed my hair in hot water, and gave it a thorough combing. Then she served me with some bread and dried fish, and I felt ready to face the world.

"Now Gaelen," she said, "you must call on Ninian's parents; Chief Nechtan and his wife Drusilla. It's the custom for new arrivals to introduce them-selves. Go up to the house and offer your greetings, Gaelen."

Leaving my bow and travelling pack in Curzen's

hut, I approached the chieftain's house. As the son of a chief, it was right that I should arrive by the front entrance, but my way was barred by a small boy seated on the balcony. On seeing me he sprang to his feet, then turned and vanished inside. By the time I'd climbed the steps he was back, brandishing a wooden short sword.

"My grandfather asks who wishes to see him!"

"I'm Gaelen," I said, "... from the waters of Fleet. I'd be grateful if you'd tell your grandfather..." I stopped short. Apolonia had appeared at the entrance, her tall graceful body clothed in a light grey gown, and with a leather belt tied loosely around her waist. Her blue eyes and easy smile enchanted me.

"Why... Gaelen's awake!" she exclaimed, "... and the sun shines fair!" Laughing, she turned to the child. "It's alright Mwynen... Gaelen's our friend. This is my son, Gaelen. Don't you think he protects us well?"

"A gallant soldier...!" I replied. The boy clung to his mother's gown, hiding his face.

"Come inside." She ushered me forward. "We've been expecting you."

Entering the cool of the reception area, I could hear the sound of music. We moved on into a large living space where a woman sat playing a harp. It was larger than the tiny instrument used by the Bard of Fleet, and with a richer quality of sound. A robust man was sitting close by, either asleep or listening intently. The music stopped and the man opened his eyes. Then they both stood up, ready to meet me.

"Father, this is Gaelen from Fleet," announced Apolonia.

"Yes, I know." Chief Nechtan advanced and placed his massive hand on my shoulder. "Many summers have passed since we last saw you... but you'll remember my wife, Drusilla?"

Drusilla was short and past her prime, but still very attractive. "How are your parents, Gaelen?" she asked.

"Ay!" added Nechtan. "How goes that old friend of mine... Latinus? Still keeping peace in the Fleet valley?"

"They're all well," I replied "But my father worries quite a lot... they keep talking about a possible invasion."

"Ah, yes! It's that cursed menace in the north." Nechtan drew himself up straight and tall. "And what's your view, Gaelen. Is the threat *real*, or the stuff of idle dreams?"

I'd been caught out before when challenged to comment on matters of conflict and war. I felt intimidated, and yet I must say *something*.

"I hunt...," I said. "To the best of my ability, I hunt."

A weak reply, but what else could I offer?

"And when I hunt, I see the animals at close range."

My mind drifted to the memory of the young deer I'd felled just a few days ago at the standing stones.

"Sometimes... just before my arrow strikes... I see the fear of violent death in their eyes. I never want to see that same look in the faces of my people... life's short, and it is best if it's not made shorter, like the deer in the forest."

"So you hunt," Nechtan persisted," and therefore have the means to *provide* for your people. But how would you provide for their *safety*?"

With Apolonia at my side I felt under pressure to respond sensibly. I was at a loss for words and I knew that she'd think me a fool. My doctrine was too simplistic... founded on sentiment. I was inclined towards the serenity of nature, where to kill cleanly for the purpose of obtaining food was right and just, but where wanton destruction was wicked and

63

offensive to all living things. But my ideas lacked maturity. Then I saw that Nechtan and Drusilla were looking beyond me, back towards the entrance, and at that moment I heard the voice of Ninian.

"Gaelen knows the right answer," he said. "It's in his heart, if not yet in his mind."

I turned to see Ninian dressed in a long grey habit, its hood drawn back to lie across his shoulders.

"It's our road-weary son!" cried Nechtan. "Come and be seated; you must tell us about your travels." He clapped his hands loudly, and Curzen appeared. "Some wine, Curzen!" The old lady bent low and retreated backwards from the room. "Drusilla," he continued, "why don't you play for us?"

Ninian was content to sit upright on a hard stool, whilst Nechtan, Apolonia and I lounged in the Roman fashion on low couches. Curzen returned, and I was soon cradling a cup of mulled wine, spiced with crushed woodruff leaves. I began to relax under the spell of Drusilla's harp.

"Where do I begin?" asked Ninian.

"You must have met with some exceptional people," said Nechtan. "Tell us about them."

"Yes; choose a hero," Drusilla smiled. "Surely you must have met with an emperor or two?"

I was amazed that she could manage to talk whilst still playing her harp.

"No, I met with no-one as great as an emperor," said Ninian. "The emperor isn't even living in Rome... he took flight last summer when the Visigoths invaded from the north. He's a young man, apparently; unintelligent and incompetent... or so I've heard."

A look of disquiet swept across Nechtan's face.

"So what's to become of the mighty empire with a *fool* for an emperor?" he asked.

"Rome is in the hands of a general," replied Ninian. "Unhappily for the empire, he's an overly ambitious soldier, wholly preoccupied with gaining control of some land to the east. In the meantime the Visigoths continue to prove troublesome... the empire's crumbling."

"And how did *you* manage to survive?" Apolonia looked concerned.

"Just as you see sister; with my body intact, and my mind sound. But most of all, with my faith in God unchanged."

This was my moment. If anyone could dispel my confusion and disbelief about the world of gods, it was Ninian.

"But what *is* your god?"

"My God is your God," replied Ninian, looking me straight in the eyes. "He made the world and every creature... every tree, within it."

"I can understand," said Nechtan, "that it simplifies things if all the gods are rolled into one. But the Druids wouldn't sympathise with that view. Nor would our Roman friends... they've been paying homage to Jupiter and Juno for centuries."

"Father's right," said Apolonia. "It would be easier to beat your head against a rock, or to plunge your hand into a serpent's nest, than to turn the Druids and the Romans around to face *your* God."

"The great Emperor Constantine turned them around... a century ago," Ninian continued. "Constantine began by worshiping the cult of the Sun before he opened his mind to Jesus Christ. He left his empire united... with a widespread belief in the Christian God."

"What made Constantine change his mind about the sun god?" I asked, still searching for the driving force behind Ninian's beliefs.

"Constantine felt the need for a *personal* saviour, Gaelen. None of the Roman gods had ever appeared on earth, so they failed to satisfy him. But God's son, Jesus, did appear on earth. Jesus Christ came to live among us just like an ordinary man, despite knowing He'd have to suffer persecution... and an agonising death."

Drusilla stopped playing and gazed anxiously at Ninian.

"All this conflict," she said, "...All this danger. Why can't people be left to worship as they please?"

"Because there's nothing so infuriating to God than the worship of false idols," Ninian replied. "It's like cutting the body of Christ into pieces."

"But what does it matter, Ninian?" asked Apolonia with a touch of exasperation in her voice. "Surely we can all live together in peace... so long as we can learn to respect one another's gods?"

"Well, that's the kind of respect that makes a calamity," replied Ninian. "Emperor Constantine died less than a hundred years ago, and already the empire is racked by division as the number of religions increases. The empire lacks the unity it once had for effective defence and government."

I remembered the Roman soldiers, all lined up on the beach at the Isle of Novantes and waiting to board their ship.

"Yes... *I've* heard that Rome's in trouble," I said. "My father and some of the other chiefs are worried that the soldiers are being called back to Rome."

Had I spoken out of turn? Ninian had gained mastery of the argument... I was sure of it. He didn't need my help.

Nechtan rose from his couch and motioned for Ninian and I to join him in the centre of the room. Placing one hand on Ninian's shoulder, the other on mine, he spoke in a kindly tone.

"The centurion who dined with us last night spoke well of you, Ninian. You've been elevated to high office by the Bishop of Rome... the Pope, no less! And we hear the Pope has appointed *you* to administer the Christian faith throughout all the land which lies north of Hadrian's great wall. The dangers we face are every bit as extreme as those you left behind in Rome. It's a heavy burden, but the time has come to give of your best."

Then, turning to me, "And you, Gaelen... will you help?"

"I'll help as best I can... if that's what Ninian wants."

Taking our leave, Ninian and I walked out onto the balcony. The sun beat down from a clear sky... not a cloud in sight.

"Father has given me permission to build a chapel," said Ninian. "We've started work preparing the ground. John and Stephen set off early this morning to look for limestone."

"Limestone...?" I muttered.

"It's a type of rock," Ninian smiled. "It can be crushed, and then used to bond stones together. When added to water it looks quite dazzling in the sunshine. We'll dress the walls in a coat of lime, Gaelen... and let God's presence shine throughout the whole of Galloway!"

Apolonia had moved silently to my side, so close that I could sense her warmth.

"Just make sure that Ninian doesn't work his Brothers too hard, Gaelen," she whispered. I felt her hand touch mine, and my spirits took flight.

CHAPTER 6

"That's the last tile!" Felix called down from the chapel roof. "You can stop mixing the mortar!"

"So we're finished!" I yelled, throwing aside my iron hammer. "Marcus! That's it...! It's the end of all the stone-crushing!"

I flexed my fingers, and winced. After several days of smashing and grinding limestone rocks into powder, my hands were blistered and sore.

Marcus dropped his wooden shovel. Pushing out his massive chest, he rested his knuckles on his hips and peered up at Felix sitting astride the apex of the chapel roof. A look of scorn swept across Marcus' face.

"Brother Felix should try some of *this* work," he grumbled. Then, turning to face me, "Felix is what they call a master craftsman, Gaelen... saw service as a builder in Rome and thinks he knows it all." As if to emphasise the point he began prodding the air in the direction of the chapel roof. "But you'll never see *him* with a spade in his hand!"

I felt sorry for Marcus. He was as strong as an ox, but I couldn't imagine him rising to the status of a master craftsman like Felix. Marcus was very physical; immensely strong, but brash and temperamental.

Felix was different. Slightly built and quietly

spoken, he was an expert at building stone walls and laying roof tiles. He'd brought iron from France, and shown me how to make a furnace using a boar skin for a bellows bag. He'd melted the iron, reshaping it to produce nails and brackets for holding the roof timbers in place.

But now the job was done, and I began to feel pride in what we'd achieved.

"We haven't done with the limestone *yet*!" called Felix, gently tapping the last roofing tile into place.

"But the roof's on!" protested Marcus. "The building's finished!"

"No it isn't; you've forgotten the cladding!" Felix replied, leaning forward to inspect his handiwork closely. "Remember what Ninian said... a coat of white to act as a beacon. Besides, limestone gives resistance to the weather!"

Marcus swore under his breath. "It'll take ages to clad the walls... I hope Bishop Ninian knows what this is doing to my hands."

With all the building activity I'd almost forgotten about Ninian. It suddenly occurred to me I hadn't seen him for days.

"Where is he?" I asked.

"Ninian...?" Marcus replied. "Meditating, I should think." He bent down to pick up his shovel again. "But don't ask me where. Nobody knows... nobody asks... and nobody cares! Don't stand there in a daze, Gaelen! We need more lime... lots of it; and don't come complaining to me about the state of your lily-white hands!"

I reached for my hammer, and brought it down heavily on another limestone boulder. The stone exploded, covering me in white dust and leaving my hands stinging more than ever with the shock of the blow. But I felt better; less flustered by Marcus' impulsive temperament.

The monotonous process went on, and I began to think of Ninian again. He'd been spending a lot of time away from Novantes. Where was he going? And why had he been so reluctant to tell anyone?

Late that night, unable to sleep, I crept out of Curzen's hut and into the pale light of the full moon. I wandered to the edge of the settlement and lay down on the grass. Closing my eyes, I took a deep breath and put my hunting instinct to the test by trying to detect the presence of the nocturnal creatures. Balor was out there somewhere... with a breeze in the right direction I might catch his scent. But the air was still. I decided to wait and see if he'd show himself.

I began to reflect on what I'd achieved since starting work with the Brothers; Felix and Marcus. I could now build in stone... reason enough to feel less ashamed about my illiteracy, immaturity and lack of sophistication. But there were also twinges of guilt. Since arriving in Novantes, working from dawn to dusk, there hadn't been time to use my bow. And that worried me. My hunting techniques were lacking practise... and not just my marksmanship. The talent for using sound and scent to track down a prey needed constant exercise.

And there was something else. I felt inside my deerskin jacket and withdrew Kaylin's parting gift... my straw Bride doll. I thought of Kaylin's fair hair, her bonny smile and lovely body. She would be waiting for me. It was my duty to return home to Fleet, to build her a house of stone and pass on my newfound skills to my father and his people. But then I'd probably never see Apolonia again. Apolonia... with her long dark hair. She was cultured too, with elegance, poise, and a gentle sense of humour. I wondered about her situation... apparently without a partner, living with her parents and two small children. I let the Bride doll fall back into my jacket... I needed to see more of Apolonia.

I'd become aware of a musty smell... borne on a chance breeze it was delicate, but quite distinct. Suddenly there was a rustle in the long grass. Balor emerged, his red and brown coat turned into a silvery grey by the light of the moon. He paused, raising his nose to sniff the air. And then, very slowly, he came towards me, his head held low... a gesture of humility and subservience? I was his saviour after all; perhaps also his soul mate. Was I about to become his night time friend...? He stopped just beyond my reach, opened his mouth and panted earnestly for a few moments. Then he appeared to recover his nerve, and advanced again. Balor, the mighty one-eyed sea god was now nuzzling close to my chest. I reached up to touch his bushy neck. He drew back sharply, turned... and was gone in an instant.

But why? He'd come so close... and then recoiled as if I'd meant to hurt him? But then I realised. Despite the loss of an eye, his senses were so much sharper than mine. He'd detected another's presence... a figure in the distance, moving briskly towards the chieftain's hut. There was no mistaking the tall lean figure of Ninian; not even with that large hood pulled up over his head. I leapt to my feet and ran towards him.

Turning, he pulled back the hood. "Gaelen...?" he whispered.

"I couldn't sleep. I was thinking... trying to decide what I should do."

"Quite right," he replied, "...Much evil is done by lack of thought. But your mind... it's *troubling* you, Gaelen... I see it in your face."

"I... I was only wondering about you," I

stammered. "We haven't seen you for a while; I was worried that's all."

"I need to be alone, Gaelen... to think." He moved closer. "To think about the enormity of what we have to achieve."

"But where do you go to be alone?"

"To a cave... by the sea; it's quite a distance from here. I used to go there as a child to throw pebbles at the waves. Now I trouble them with my questions... and my nightmares."

"And to talk with the Christ God...?"

"Yes, of course I turn to Him... for guidance in deciding what I have to do."

"Marcus doesn't talk to the Christ God."

Even as I spoke I was wishing I'd kept silent. It wasn't in my nature to malign another man. True, Marcus wasn't the easiest of people to get along with, and certainly he seemed less pious than the other Brothers. But it wasn't for me to convey as much to Ninian. Besides, I'd grown fond of Marcus, despite his bad temper.

"Believe me," said Ninian, smiling faintly. "Brother Marcus prays well enough. He prayed hard before we sailed from France. Come to think of it, he didn't stop praying until we'd reached the safety of Novantes... he's terrified of the sea. No... Marcus is a good man, Gaelen; a good worker too. And he talks with God... quietly, in his own mind."

"Your plan... your mission... is it dangerous, as your parents said?"

"Somewhat." Ninian sighed deeply. "If I learned anything at all in Rome, it's that a barbarian race will always find excuses to hold fast to their pagan beliefs."

"You mean the Picts?"

"The Picts, the Visigoths, the Huns and all the

others... but the Picts especially. They detest the Romans. The Picts have battled hard against the Roman legions for centuries, whilst we Galloway folk have been content to enjoy Roman protection. We've traded with the Romans... we've even sent our men into battle on the side of the Romans. Yes, it will be a dangerous mission... we can expect no mercy from the Picts."

He scanned my face as if to study my reaction, and I began to feel nervous.

"How good is the Christ God's protection in battle?" I asked. "Is he as good as the war god, Lugh... does he repair broken swords and lances? Our Druid said that Lugh can make slain warriors come back the next day, unhurt and ready to be killed again."

"It all depends on what God wants to achieve." Ninian seemed amused. "Let's just hope that we have God on our side, aye Gaelen? Tell me... do you fear death?"

"No..." I swallowed hard. "Not if it's quick."

"Some men fear it," he continued. "...Just as children fear the dark. But it's the people whom the dead leave behind that suffer most. Apolonia, for instance, she has yet to recover from the death of her husband."

So Apolonia had no husband! I felt a wave of exhilaration... she was accessible! But my excitement was mixed with compassion. Was she ready to build a new relationship, I wondered?

"What happened to Apolonia's husband?"

"Killed in the north two summers ago... trying to strike a blow against the Picts. Too many of our men have gone off to fight alongside the Roman army. Too many have given their lives... and all for what? The threat still hangs over us despite all the killing. We shall have to find another way."

73

He placed a hand on my shoulder.

"But you're tired, Gaelen. You must sleep. I'll speak with you again... when the chapel's finished."

He turned to go, but hesitated.

"Have you met with Plebius yet?" he asked.

"Plebius...? No, I don't know him."

"You should... he's a fine young man... and rather fond of Apolonia."

My heart began to sink. Was she already pledged to another?

"Plebius's father is an elder in another village," Ninian went on. But even as he was speaking, the words had little meaning as I struggled to overcome my deep sense of disappointment. "Try to meet Plebius when he's next in Novantes... you'll like him. I'm told he's an excellent marksman!"

I strolled slowly back to Curzen's hut. Was this, then, to be my fate... to live the life of a second rate suitor? First my brother, favoured as the right man for Kaylin. And now another man pursuing Apolonia... a supreme bowman named Plebius. Was I to become like Marcus, with no special accomplishments apart from an ability to crush rocks and mix mortar? I was becoming an outsider... a feeble bystander. I knew that I wouldn't sleep that night, or for several nights to come.

*****

The task of mixing plaster to clad the walls left Marcus and I covered in white slime. Days went by, my mind almost numb with boredom, but eventually the job was done.

I raised myself up to wipe the grime from my face, blinking away the perspiration and lime powder which stung my eyes. Something had caught my attention, and as my vision cleared I saw two figures approaching.

Marcus had also spotted them.

"Hah...!" Marcus exclaimed. "It's John and Stephen! They're coming to inspect our work!" He sounded bitter as he handed the last bucket of lime plaster to Felix. "I expect they've been out spreading the Gospel... no time for *real* work!"

"Marcus...!" John cried out. "God *will* be proud of you!" He was motioning towards the chapel. "But then, how could you possibly fail Him with that heroic-looking body of yours?"

Marcus just nodded, grinning wryly.

As they came closer I noticed Stephen gazing down at my bare white-splattered arms and legs.

"And here's proof of *another* good worker," he said. "...Lime slime!"

I looked up at the breathtaking structure I'd helped to create, magnificent and dazzling in the brilliant sunshine.

"It was worth the effort," I replied.

Felix held an upturned leather bucket at arms length and banged its sides to empty some dregs of lime-wash onto the grass.

"The chapel's yours, Brothers," he said. "Make good use of it." Then he turned to me. "And we won't forget your contribution, Gaelen. You're not one of us, but you deserve much of the credit."

"I think he deserves a good bath," added Stephen.

I felt a rush of blood to my face; it was good to be acknowledged, but I was embarrassed.

"If we're finished," I said, "I'll go and get cleaned up."

"Go with God then," smiled Felix. "And try not to frighten the ducks!"

I spent a long time at the village pond, washing the

lime from my body. I stood up at last, slipped into my deerskin jacket, and began the weary walk back towards Curzen's hut.

Suddenly, my legs were struck from behind. There was a gasp, and I spun round to see a small boy lying winded on the ground. A ball rolled away towards a little girl standing close by. She was covering her mouth, giggling.

"Mwynen...! Fionn...!" a woman cried out. It was Apolonia... she was running towards us. "Why don't you look where you're going...? Stupid children! Mwynen... say sorry to poor Gaelen."

"I'm fine," I said, stooping forward to help the boy to his feet. "...But what about the brave warrior?"

Mwynen smiled self-consciously, murmured an apology, and ran off to play ball with his sister.

"I'm so sorry." Apolonia looked slightly flushed. "You'll be exhausted... is the work finished?"

I nodded. "It's all done."

"Share some fruit drink with us, then."

Was I dreaming? For the past few nights I'd lain awake fantasising about being with this woman. Time and time again I'd lapsed into fitful sleep, only to find myself immersed in nightmares, ridiculed by Ninian for imagining that I could aspire to someone like Apolonia, even if there were no Plebius.

"You must join us," she urged. "There's someone I want you to meet."

She led the way as we mounted the steps. A young man appeared on the balcony, and I knew that I must brace myself for what was to come. He was taller than I, good looking, and dressed in a new deerskin jacket. I felt shabby by comparison.

"This is Plebius, Gaelen," said Apolonia. "Plebius, this is Gaelen... hunter and builder... the son of Chief Latinus of Fleet."

"I've been hearing about you," smiled Plebius, clasping my hand. "And congratulations... that's a magnificent building you've put up."

"I had little to do with it... it's all the work of Ninian and his men."

I was resolved to say little; resigned to begin the journey home to Fleet without further delay.

"Here, Gaelen." Apolonia handed me a drink. "It's fresh... I made it this morning."

I swallowed greedily... it tasted like honey.

"Apolonia tells me you're a bowman," said Plebius. His eyes darted from my head to my feet and then back again, looking me up and down as if I were a poor outcast... an inferior.

"Not a good one," I replied.

There was an awkward silence.

"They say I'm quite good with the slingshot," he went on. "Do you shoot competitively?"

"I think Gaelen is a hunter," said Apolonia softly.

"I don't shoot against other bowmen." I replied. "Only by myself. I sometimes use a leather ball for a target... it helps to improve my accuracy."

I felt a gentle nudge at my leg, and looked down to see young Mwynen gazing up into my face.

"I want to see Gaelen shoot," he smiled.

"Not now, Mwynen," said Apolonia. "Gaelen's tired... he's been working hard..."

"Yes," interrupted Plebius, "but shooting is a pastime, Apolonia. It's not supposed to be tedious, like working." His eyes remained fixed on mine, as if rooting out my competitive instincts. "I'll shoot, if you will Gaelen."

I'd never seen a sling shot, and was curious. Besides, what had I to lose? Work on the chapel was finished, and I'd soon be going home... back to Kaylin and my hunting. So why not start practising now?

"All right..." I placed my empty cup on the table. "Where do we shoot?"

"Over there will do."

He pointed towards an open area at the edge of the settlement, and then reached down to unhook a small leather pouch from his belt.

"What's in there?" I asked.

"Sling stones! Get your bow... I'll see you at the clearing. And don't forget to bring your leather ball!"

Back in Curzen's hut I found the target ball in my travelling pack. I'd left my bow unstrung to remove the strain from its shaft. Now, pressing down with all my weight to establish the curvature, I slipped the gut string into the notches at each end. My bow was taught and ready for action. With the ball in one hand, my bow and quiver in the other, I set off to meet my challenger.

"What distance do you shoot?" I called.

"Twenty paces... perhaps a little more!" replied Plebius. And then he continued, "But that's a very small target!"

"*Fifty* paces, then!" I was feeling good with my bow in my hand, and I knew that I could strike a chicken's eye at fifty paces.

Whilst pacing out the distance I became aware that a crowd was beginning to assemble. Should I have agreed to this? Though a good marksman, shooting for me was a solitary affair... my mind had to be focussed, without the distraction of a critical audience. I reached fifty paces, found a pointed stick, and drove it into the ground with the ball mounted on top. Then I strolled back to the firing line which Plebius had marked between two upright poles.

"We're gathering a few spectators!" Plebius sounded confident and in full command of his faculties. "It's your target, Gaelen... go ahead and shoot."

With the bow in my left hand, I turned to face the tiny ball. Taking an arrow from the quiver, I clipped its notched end to my bowstring. Then, slowly raising the bow, I drew back my right arm until my thumb was firmly locked under my chin.

But there was something badly wrong! It just didn't feel right... the load was excessive, and I couldn't hold a steady aim! I was out of condition... the strength in my drawing arm waning.

Nor was my mind properly focussed. Apolonia would be watching, and I was about to suffer the greatest humiliation of my life. I *must* stay focussed... try to concentrate on the target! With no crosswind to create a sideways drift, I only had to align my arrow directly with the ball... and then to get the elevation right. My arms were trembling as I felt a breath of wind in my face... elevate upwards a little more to counteract the headwind... there!

Off went the arrow, and I knew at the instant of release that it would miss. I'd failed to muster the strength and absolute concentration required to strike a target at fifty paces.

"Good try," said Plebius, "... pretty close."

The sling was already primed and swaying gently from his right hand as he studied the target. Then it was in motion around his head, the sound increasing in pitch as it spun faster and faster. I lay down on the grass for safety... a strike in the head from that projectile would have meant certain death. Then, with a snap, the stone was released.

I heard a dull thud, followed by a muffled thump as my leather ball fell to the ground. I was awestruck. Amidst applause from the crowd I stood up and stepped forward to offer my praise.

"A great shot, Plebius... I hadn't realised the power

79

of the slingshot... an impressive weapon in the right hands... congratulations."

"A great shot?" he laughed. "A *good* one maybe, but hardly a great one... I only wanted to set the ball spinning, Gaelen!"

I could imagine what was to come... sympathetic looks from the people who'd come to watch us... hollow words of commiseration. They were a kindly folk, but this wasn't my scene. I would leave straight away; say my farewells quickly, and head for home. I turned to recover my target ball.

Then I heard a man's voice calling my name. Glancing back I saw Ninian approaching.

"Gaelen... Plebius...!" he called again. "A word with you both...!"

He drew us together, resting a hand on each of our shoulders and speaking quickly.

"My journey north begins tomorrow. I've sought God's advice... and I want you both to come with me."

"But your Brothers...," said Plebius.

"The Brothers must stay," interrupted Ninian. "There is much for them to do in Novantes. I've spoken with them, and they've agreed that both of you should accompany me. But the mission will be hazardous. I'm ready to accept your refusal, and will think no worse of either of you for deciding not to join me."

"If Gaelen goes, then so will I," Plebius beamed.

I was trembling with exhilaration, and elated beyond all imagination. I hoped it wouldn't show... I must appear cool, like Plebius.

"I told you before... I'm ready," I said.

"Tomorrow then... and prepare for an early start!" Ninian turned away with Plebius, and they both moved off to mingle with the crowd.

I had to be alone to think about the implications of

what Ninian had asked me to do. Securing the bow across my shoulders, I retrieved my target ball and wayward arrow. Then I strolled out of the village and headed towards the evening sun, my eyes watering as I gazed into its intense brightness.

With Novantes well behind me, I found a comfortable patch of grass beside a stream, lay back, and relaxed to the sound of water rippling over the smooth pebbles. Birdsong filled my consciousness. There was a swish of air close to my face... the swallows were busy, swooping fast and low over the grass in pursuit of insects rising in the warm air.

Something stirred in the grass behind me. I lay still, trying to imagine what it might be. Balor...? The rustling stopped, and then began again, but louder. My instincts were at their sharpest as I realised that this was no wild animal, but another human being. I sat upright and turned to confront the intruder. It was Apolonia!

She came steadily closer and I felt my heart pounding... the surge of blood deafening as it accelerated through my veins. Was this really happening? She moved gracefully, and seated herself on the grass beside me. I leaned towards her, unable to speak, and touched her breasts lightly. In one fluid movement she lay back, stretched herself out, and reached up to touch my forehead, her cool fingers moving slowly down across my eyelids, until her hand rested against my cheek.

"I'm disappointed," she said, smiling tenderly. "...To think that you could leave us without even saying goodbye to me."

Her hand moved again, gently round to the back of my neck, tightening its grip and easing me down... down to her lovely face... her misty eyes... her mouth.

Our union was wild and frenzied, my craving

unrestrained. Apolonia, on reaching her moment of extreme pleasure, let out a cry... like the release of a deep frustration... the liberation of a repressed fury... a sense of longing for her dead husband, perhaps. We lay together until the light faded, and I was deeply in love.

CHAPTER 7

I'd lost count of the number of days we'd been walking. The order was always the same... single file with Ninian in the lead, then Plebius, and me at the rear.

We'd stayed with a family of crofters last night. Even now I could feel the dizzying effects of that stupefying mix of honey and water with which they'd repeatedly filled our bellies. Maybe I shouldn't have drunk so much. But Plebius had taken it all in his stride and I hadn't wanted to seem inferior. By the end of the third offering I'd felt at the edge of a new world. I'd stood at the threshold of a wonderland of feasting and pleasure, where apple trees were always in fruit; one pig always alive and another freshly roasted, where there was no grief, and where the people's hair was flecked with gold. Had I reached the brink of the otherworld? Our Druid had often told of gods exiled to that place... gods who'd liked it so much they never returned. But I was mortal, and the gods of the other-world had returned me to the real world. Now my head was aching as we walked in the sweltering heat of a mid-day sun.

Ninian set a lively pace despite the uncomfortable heat. I wriggled my shoulders and upper body, trying to ventilate the inside of my deerskin jacket. Some early morning rain had left the ferns and grasses saturated, and they were lashing uncomfortably around my legs.

There was something weird about this place we were passing through... those woodlands on either side were dark and forbidding. Seeking reassurance, I reached up and touched the bow slung over my shoulder, then the quiver of arrows at my side. I was prepared... but for what?

Plebius glanced back at me over his shoulder.

"It's unfair, Gaelen... don't you think?"

"What do you mean? What's unfair...?"

"Last night... at the crofter's hut... you and I wearing the finest of deerskin jackets, whilst Ninian in that simple grey garb manages to get all the attention!"

He was right. Last night, the children had been fascinated and delighted by Ninian's unconventional dress. The crofters would accept no reward for their generosity, content only to listen to Ninian talking about the Christ God and of life in far away places.

"Perhaps it's something to do with the stories he tells." I glanced ahead to see if Ninian was listening. But he was silent as he strode purposefully forward. I wondered how stifled he must have felt under that long rough gown.

Ever since leaving Novantes we'd been made welcome at every isolated farming community along the way. We'd shared their meagre suppers and listening to their stories of hardship. Wintertime could be cruel this far north, and Mother Earth a mean provider.

I began to reflect on the people we'd met over the past few days. I'd detected a change in their mood... an increasing level of anxiety, the further north we'd ventured. Now I considered it, today we'd encountered not a single man, woman or child.

My thoughts were interrupted by a howling from a long way off... then I heard it again. Plebius stopped and turned round to face me.

"Wolf?" He looked puzzled.

"Wild dog, anyway," I replied. We stood quietly, listening; but that was the last we heard. Then, realising that Ninian was leaving us behind, Plebius turned and rushed after him. I followed.

Such cries were rare during the day. And there was something symbolic about that sound... a sense of urgency, not like the ritual and melancholy baying of a wolf. Could it have been a moor hound signalling danger to its mate, perhaps?

Plebius was talking again, and disturbing my concentration.

"What did you think of the people... last night?"

"The crofters...? They were a bit tense and nervous. I don't remember what happened... not after the drinking started."

"That's because you drank too much," Plebius laughed. "We lost touch with you, Gaelen." Then after a pause, "I felt sorry for those people, though. You only had to mention the word 'Pict' and they'd turn quite pale. No wonder they've taken to drinking that... what did Ninian call it... the honeyed dew of paradise? One little sip and life becomes very agreeable. How's your head, by the way?"

Ninian signalled a stop before I could reply. The narrow winding track we'd been following was about to join a wider and more substantial road.

"That's our way ahead," said Ninian, pointing towards the north. "It's a Roman road... see how straight it is? It was probably used years ago by the legions marching up towards the Antonine Wall."

"Overgrown too," I murmured.

What might once have been a good road was now

covered in a tangle of bush and thicket. As before, the forest loomed close on either side. But it was the very straightness of this road which seemed to present an even greater risk of ambush; any bandit would see us coming from a long way off.

"We'll soon be at the Clyde," Ninian continued. "Then, if our information's correct, we'll be close to Cadder with the Campsie Fells beyond."

"Who controls these parts?" asked Plebius.

"No-one knows for sure." Ninian withdrew a cloth from his sleeve and dabbed the perspiration from his face. "Chief Cadoc was the Overlord at Cadder. He once came to Novantes when I was very young. I can still remember him... a great man." Ninian tucked the cloth back into his sleeve. "But that was long before the Legions withdrew from this area. If Cadoc has survived, he'll be very old now."

I could imagine the waves of Pictish warriors storming across the Antonine Wall and following hard on the heels of the retreating Romans; I'd heard that Picts never miss an opportunity to capture more land. But my daydreaming was cut short.

"Look!" cried Plebius, pointing ahead, "...Coming out of the woods!"

There were two people... a man and a small boy. The man appeared unsteady; he was leaning forward, led by the child, and covering his face with his free hand. Moving slowly and hesitantly through the undergrowth, they both looked shaken. On reaching the road, they turned and came towards us.

"Their clothes," I gasped, "... they're blood-stained!"

Ninian called out to them, "Are you all right...? What's happened...?"

They stopped abruptly.

"Leave us alone!" the man cried hoarsely. He

seemed unwell and there was a look of despair about him. Still shielding his eyes, he reached out and pulled the boy closer to his side. I wanted to be nearer... to offer support.

The boy took a step forward and tried to speak.

"My father... It's my father's..." but his voice wavered and his words died away as he broke down in tears.

The man was now clawing aimlessly at the air, as if desperately trying to retrieve the boy. Reunited, they turned together and without another word staggered back into the forest. I felt shocked and bewildered.

"The boy... he was trying to tell us something," said Ninian. "Did you hear?"

"He was too upset." Plebius shook his head. "It might have been anything. But I think the man was his father. Shouldn't we go after them?"

"No... leave them be." Ninian's mood seemed to have changed to one of indifference.

"But we frightened them!" exclaimed Plebius. "And we need to know why!"

"He's right," I said. "I think we should go after them, if only to show we meant no harm. There was blood... and I think the man was blind. He needs help."

"Not now...!" There was an anger and bluntness about Ninian's voice I'd never heard before. "We'll know soon enough!"

Feeling resentful, I eased the strap of my travelling pack off my shoulder to relieve its weight. And then we were walking again... in silence. The harmony which had existed between us since leaving Novantes had soured.

The incident left a feeling of emptiness inside me. We'd let those people down. If only I'd stood my ground against Ninian. I'd still so much to learn, like mastering the skill of argument; to put my case firmly, however clever and influential the opposition... and then, importantly, to keep to my convictions.

Ninian's pace was very rapid now, making it impossible for me to read the signals that would have helped to form a mental image of our surroundings. I needed more time to absorb the sounds and scents of the woodland. Left to myself I'd have stopped occasionally to allow the darkest recesses of the forest to yield up their secrets. That man... his face. There was evil at work, and I wanted to track it down.

Deliberately, I turned my mind to happier memories of home... of those carefree days of hunting in the hills, and my frequent visits to the standing stones to be silent and alone. I'd matured a lot since then. I'd learned to work as part of a team, and even to bear with the complaining Marcus. I wasn't a loner any more. Since leaving Novantes with Ninian and Plebius I'd learned that the secret of forming true friendships is to live closely with one's companions; to eat and sleep in their company out in the open.

But did they know about my feelings for Apolonia... that I'd made love to her? Plebius was fond of Apolonia. Should I open my mind to him? I'd experienced the pain of jealousy for myself, and wouldn't wish it upon another man. No... so long as Plebius had no access to my thoughts then we'd surely remain friends. A great deal of the world is invisible to us, and sometimes it's best not to search into inaccessible places.

Suddenly we'd stopped again. I reacted too late and careered into the back of Plebius. There was a shuffling sound, then a blur of activity! We were being surrounded... by a gang of thugs! There were ten or more, some with faces painted blue! I'd allowed my guard to slip, and we'd been caught unawares. I reached for my bow but my arms were seized from behind. My bow, travelling pack and quiver were snatched away, and my elbows drawn back and fastened tightly behind me, stretching the sinews and muscles in my shoulders until I gasped with pain. I struggled, twisting one way and then the other, but to no avail. Some of the gang had gripped me tightly from behind.

"A fine looking chicken!" sneered one, spinning me round to face him. As he ran his eyes over my helpless body, a convulsion stirred in my gut.

I scanned the gang's weaponry; an assortment of bows, spears, swords and knives. I began to shiver uncontrollably. There was only one explanation... we'd been entrapped by a Pict raiding party.

I glanced first at Plebius. His arms were being bound together across his chest. And then at Ninian... one of the gang was raising a fist over Ninian's head!

"He's not armed!" I screamed.

But the fist descended. Ninian reeled under the blow, falling to his knees.

I felt a storm of rage surging up inside me. I wasn't afraid any more; I was past that. Another strike and Ninian would be finished... he must be protected! I lurched forward, my elbows locked behind me, but Ninian's assailant barred my way. There was a sharp metallic sound as he drew a blade from its scabbard... a Roman short sword!

"Stay back, Gaelen...!" Ninian's voice sounded weak.

"I'll slay *this* one now!" The blue faced barbarian stared hard into my face as he advanced swiftly towards me, weighing the sword in his hand.

I closed my eyes and held my breath. That blade... it would be closing on me! Where would it strike? And how would it feel? Would it come as a slashing blow... crashing through my bones? Or would it be thrust into my guts... slicing its way upwards, severing my organs and spilling my life's juices?

There was a sound... not the noise of a scything blade, but a soft pounding, rapid and rhythmic, like a fast moving animal covering the ground at speed. I heard a wild and savage growl, followed by the panic-stricken cry of a man.

I opened my eyes... my assailant lay on the ground, pinioned by a writhing moor hound, its red and brown coat trembling with strain as it tore relentlessly at the ruffian's face and throat. The gang seemed frozen, unsure of how to respond.

"Balor...!" I yelled.

The growling changed to a soulful whine as the hound continued to wreak havoc on the man's body. Balor was responding to my call... communicating his resolve to liberate me from this loathsome monster, the imbecile who'd planned to end my life.

Then I heard another sound... the swish of an arrow. Balor's head reared up as the shaft plunged deep into his powerful bushy neck. Pictish blood and gore trailed from his open jaws as a second arrow followed, striking his side with a hollow thwack. Against all the pain, he turned and peered into my face with that solitary eye, touching me with his thoughts.

"Didn't you hear me, Gaelen," he seemed to say, "... I cried out... I tried to warn you!"

Then, with the sparkle fading from his eye, he rolled slowly onto his side. Balor, remote and unobtrusive, yet steadfast and self-sacrificing, was giving up his life... for me... his true friend. By that single act of supreme bravery, he'd shown these brutes the meaning of *real* courage and daring. They deserved to die many agonising deaths before their final annihilation, but Balor... he would die only once.

I bade him farewell in my heart as his soul hastened to the land of the gods.

I saw Ninian making a determined effort to stand. He tottered for a moment and nearly fell, but regained his composure.

"Harm these men," he exclaimed hoarsely, "and your king will be greatly offended!" He swept his eyes over the gang. "Believe me; I know that your king will be pitiless in his revenge on any who tries to prevent me from keeping my appointment with him!"

Was this a trick? Ninian had never mentioned a Pictish king. The gang remained transfixed. Were they disturbed by what Ninian had just said, or were they still in shock over the sudden appearance of Balor and his ruthless attack on their comrade?

One of them, thickset and with the appearance of a leader motioned for the gang to lower their weaponry. Then he moved forward and knelt beside Balor's victim. The wretched man was still breathing... or trying to. Scarlet bubbles were forming in a deep yawning cavern that was once his throat. The leader drew a dagger, raised it up and brought it firmly down, sinking it up to the hilt in the man's chest. There was a wheezing sound, loud at first, but fading away to nothing. The flow of blooded froth from under the victim's mangled chin eased... and finally ceased.

The leader rose to his feet and strode menacingly towards Ninian.

"And yet," said Ninian, his voice now stronger, "I might still convince your king that you acted well, and with his best interests at heart!"

The leader stopped within a dagger's strike, and gazed at Ninian as if astonished by the sight of this strange yet inoffensive looking man, dressed only in a plain hooded gown.

"Your friends..." continued Ninian, nodding

towards the gang, "...They obviously have a healthy regard for the power and ferocity of their king." Then, looking back into the face of their leader, "And they'll have more respect for you... if you'll only use your wits to help keep them alive."

The leader turned to look at his followers. Then he glanced at Plebius and me, as if searching for a weakness... an excuse for another killing? Had Ninian been too outspoken? Had he gone too far? I was weak with the fear of being run-through with that fearsome dagger... to have the blood of a Pict mingling with my own. Striding over to one of his party, the leader snatched up my bow and advanced towards me waving it in the air.

"Lickspittle chicken...!" he yelled, shaking the bow in my face. "It'll take more than *this* to save you from King Tudwell!" He pressed the tip of the bow firmly against my neck, forcing me to raise my chin. "Die slowly, chicken... learn how it feels to have Tudwell give the order to have the flesh stripped from your writhing bones!" He jerked his head towards the forest.

A thump in my back left me gasping. I was being jostled off the road and into the undergrowth. Glancing back, I saw Ninian and Plebius being hustled into line behind me.

We moved swiftly along a narrow track. I ducked and weaved to avoid the low-growing thorns and holly bushes, struggling to keep my balance as jagged tree roots and dead branches caught at my feet. I must slacken the pace, or risk a fall. To stumble now, with my arms trussed behind me, was almost unthinkable; the pain in my arms was already severe. I slowed a little.

"Move, swine...!" Another blow to my back... I almost fell. "Move... or I'll separate your ribs!"

Something sharp was being jabbed into my spine, and I felt another blow between the shoulders. I shook my head vigorously, trying to rid my brow of sweat.

"The chicken's shedding water!" yelled my follower. I blinked again as my eyes filled with tears.

"Not for long," somebody laughed, "... not after we've skinned him alive!"

I sensed the nearness of death... an obnoxious smell... the stinking carcass of a dead animal; or so I thought. But the smell grew stronger until the air reeked with the stench of smoke and decaying flesh. I closed my mouth, breathing in short bursts through my nose.

We'd arrived at the edge of a large clearing, and although the fetid air told the story, nothing could have prepared me for the full horror of what confronted us. I was thrust forward again and saw circles of smouldering ash; all that remained of some village huts. A goat stood tethered to a pole... trembling and bleating pathetically. Some chickens strutted hesitantly, warily... and strangely silent.

Worse was to come... human remains... naked, torn, and hung carelessly across the bars of a wooden fence. The women had been slashed, the men gutted. Two infants had been dismembered and left to die, the misery of their final agony etched into their tiny faces. I lowered my head, and felt more tears mingling with the sweat in my eyes.

According to Ninian's teaching, my sense of grief was misplaced. Hadn't he once said that death itself was nothing to be frightened about, and that we must focus our minds on the living... to be attentive towards those whom the dead leave behind? No-one had been left behind here. No-one had survived. Therefore, according to Ninian's reasoning, there was no reason for me to shed tears.

But these people had every right to live. Who knows what wonders those children may have aspired to... what skills attained and services rendered... what acts of bravery? Our future had been deprived of them, of their offspring, and of all of the countless generations of families they might have spawned; warm and good-natured people, with the resolve to bring beauty and order back into this world of villainy, fear and appalling suffering.

"Eingel...!" someone called out from behind. "Look what we've found!"

I blinked away my tears and glanced round to see more barbarians emerging from the woodland. They were using spears to jostle more prisoners... a man and a small boy... the two we'd seen on the road earlier!

Startled by a thick guttural voice, I spun my head back to the front.

"You see chicken... nobody escapes from Eingel!"

The gang leader was standing so close that I was forced to inhale his loathsome breath.

"Nobody...!" he wheezed. "I always track them down in the end!"

He leaned closer and I held my breath to avoid ingesting the foul stench.

"Those two..." he said, nodding towards the man and boy. "I put the old man's eyes out this morning... then left him alone for a while... just enough time for him to realise he was going to die. Very considerate of me, don't you think?"

Now I began to understand the events which had led to our encounter with the couple on the road. Somehow, the young boy must have managed to rescue his father from a certain death... I recalled the terror in the man's voice when we'd called out to them.

"A brave lad that," continued Eingel. "...A pity

about his spineless father, though."

"Eingel...!" came another call. "What are we going to do with these two?"

"Spare them, Eingel!" cried Ninian, stepping forward. "Take me instead... I'll surrender my meeting with King Tudwell in exchange for their lives."

Eingel peered down at the ground and stroked the rough stubble on his chin for several moments as if trying to weigh the options. Then he glanced towards the father and child before turning back to face Ninian.

"No, not you man of rags," he said at last. "We'll leave Tudwell to decide your fate. Bring the boy here!"

I heard a heartrending commotion behind me and could only imagine the scene; a father and son, the remnants of a loving family... the sole survivors of a whole village. Now even they were to be parted.

The boy was dragged forward to be held firmly in Eingel's grasp. I looked down at the child's tearstained face. This was real terror... the zenith of his suffering. Surely there was nothing more that Eingel could do to intensify his grief... to deepen his sense of loss.

"What's it to be, Eingel?" The voice from behind sounded impatient.

"Go on then!" Eingel yelled back. "Examine the omens!"

There was a pause, and then my blood ran cold as the air was pierced by an appalling shriek of pain. Then a moment's silence... a low moaning, followed by a laboured gasp... then silence again. My eyes remained fixed on the boy, his face white and death-like; no more tears... just emptiness.

"The omens are favourable!" someone called. "His intestines have a healthy look!"

"Then my judgement was sound!" Eingel clasped the boy's head between his massive hands. "The child's courage has been rewarded... he shall live!" Then he turned to Ninian. "And the gods are pleased that I've spared you, man of rags... for an agony much worse than you can ever imagine!"

CHAPTER 8

How much further we'd marched after witnessing that scene of brutality earlier in the day was beyond my comprehension, but I was fast approaching the limit of my endurance. Sheer exhaustion would have prevented me from noticing that we'd entered a vast settlement had it not been for the noisy crowd of onlookers which had grown around us. They looked primitive, some with their faces and limbs painted blue, many with scarred cheeks.

The incessant shoving and jabbing in my back began to ease... I slowed my pace and came at last to a standstill.

"Hold them!" Eingel scowled. He turned away and bounded up several steps, then disappeared through a doorway on the balcony of a large hut.

I heard the sound of movement behind me... the crowd was pressing closer. There were females amongst them, but not of Celtic stock. These women had a rough look, their hair dyed red and accentuating their wild appearance.

"Cadder has fallen," Ninian whispered. "...To the Picts."

Eingel's men had left Ninian's hands free, but he looked very ashen after that earlier blow to his head.

Plebius stood at Ninian's side, his arms still fastened across his chest.

I saw the young boy tethered by a rope to one of Eingel's men. The child was gazing vacantly at the mob, as if his mind had been stretched beyond caring. He glanced towards me, and I forced a smile. There was a faint movement around his mouth... perhaps the ghost of a smile in return.

I tried moving my shoulders, but a stab of pain swept across my back. This was no way to face my end; trussed-up and without the means of self defence!

"Behold your King!" Eingel had reappeared on the balcony. "Tudwell... Lord of Cadder and Strathclyde!"

First the tyrannical bully, and now the grovelling liegeman, Eingel was announcing the imminent appearance of his Pictish master. He stood aside as the king emerged... an awesome sight as he towered over his diminutive henchman.

Tudwell moved slowly to the edge of the balcony, and the crowd erupted.

"Hail mighty King...! Tudwell...! Warlord...! Conqueror...!"

The king raised his hand casually and the adulation quickly subsided.

His outer garment, a long red cloak, was lavishly embroidered with tracery and precious regalia. I'd seen similar cloaks worn by the most senior Roman soldiers as they relaxed off duty. The cloak lay open at the front to reveal a leather battledress beneath, like the one worn by my father. Sunlight glinted from a cluster of gold and silver chains fastened loosely around his neck and shoulders. The whole effect was baffling... a haphazard mix of Celtic and Roman wear... the spoils of war, no doubt.

I glanced at Tudwell's suntanned face... it bore the stamp of a tough and assertive leader, but there was little joy in his expression. He looked miserable, as if plagued by the memory of some past tragedy. His eyes swept slowly over us he descended the balcony steps.

Then he approached Ninian.

"So...!" boomed Tudwell in a deep voice. "...*This* is the man of rags!"

He reached out to examine Ninian's gown. After fingering the material for a few moments he raised the hood to show the crowd.

"There, you see...!" he grinned. "Your king has become a host to beggar men!" A ripple of laughter spread through the mob.

He let the hood fall and turned to me.

I trembled and felt faint as he approached and stood close to me, studying my face. I thought I might lose consciousness. But he turned away at last and moved towards Plebius.

"Eingel...!" Tudwell yelled, scouring the mob for his gang leader.

"My lord...?" I heard Eingel clattering down the balcony steps.

"These men... have they been searched?"

"Yes, my lord! One of them had a bow!"

"But did you examine them again... *thoroughly*?" Tudwell rapped out. "...Before bringing them to me?"

A look of dread crossed Eingel's face.

"A second time...?" his voice faltered. "No..." He fell silent under Tudwell's contemptuous gaze.

"This one...," Tudwell pointed at Plebius. "There's something concealed in his jacket!"

Eingel reacted instantly. He bore down upon Plebius, tore open his jacket and seized the sling and ammunition pouch which lay between Plebius's trussed arms. Eingel drew a deep breath as he gazed down at the tiny leather bundle. His expression changed swiftly from one of disbelief to that of a man in extreme peril.

"Bring it!" snapped Tudwell.

Eingel sped to the king's side and handed over the sling.

"I've seen this weapon before," said Tudwell thoughtfully, turning the sling over in his hands. "But I've never seen it used. It's fortunate that it wasn't a knife... aye, Eingel?"

Eingel scowled at his gang, as if desperate to re-establish his authority and intent on finding someone else to blame for his oversight.

Then I heard Ninian's voice breaking the tense silence.

"I've heard that great kings who know goodness from evil rest easy in their beds, and rise early in the morning to be greater still. But you my lord... you carry a troubled conscience."

I knew from the way Tudwell glowered at Ninian that we'd been brought one step closer to the brink of death. I felt like a helpless child, quaking with fear and unable to think... I would plead for a quick end.

"Is that so, man of rags?" Tudwell's voice grew steadily louder. "...You dare to construe the workings of my mind, then? You have the effrontery to doubt my wisdom... my authority!" He was turning crimson with rage. "Yes...!" he bellowed. "This king is troubled... but not for *himself*! He motioned towards the crowd. "This king is troubled for the lives of his *people*!"

There came a deafening roar as the crowd went wild. Slogans of loyalty were followed by a succession of demands. "Cut out their guts...! Examine the signs...! Burn them alive...! Pound their bones...!" I heard a woman crying out. "Make them drink their own blood first!" she shrieked.

Tudwell appeared to regain some of his earlier composure. Again he raised his hand and commanded instant silence.

"If only you had half a brain, man of rags," he declared, shaking his head. "Then you would know that a king's conscience is never still... I have merely to *declare* war. It's my *people* who must suffer in the aftermath... the young warrior who must fight and die!"

He looked down at the sling and studied it for a few more moments.

"We must see how this thing works!" he cried, pitching the sling onto the ground in front of Plebius. "Cut him loose! Prepare a shootout... two on two... just one shot each!"

"Gwion!" yelled Eingel.

A small man rushed forward, his face twisted into a villainous smile by a terrible battle scar.

"Untie him!" Eingel was pointing at me. "Give him a bow!"

Gwion ran behind me and cut my elbows free. Exquisite pain...! The blood of life flowing back into my arms! I reached out, and once again felt my bow firmly in my grasp.

"You two!" rasped Eingel, motioning towards Plebius and me. "You two will *stay* put... one movement from either of you and the man of rags will die!"

Then he turned to Gwion.

"Find somewhere at one hundred paces." He pointed to a spot at the edge of the forest. "Over there!"

Gwion set off obediently. Eingel lingered, his mouth widening into sinister grin.

"We get to shoot first," he sneered. "And remember... keep still! When you're both dead, we'll harden your brains with lime and turn them into magic stone!"

Hissing with laughter, he coughed up the filthy

contents of his phlegm-filled lungs and spat the foul brew at my feet.

"And if by some accident you *do* manage to survive," he wheezed, "you can return the fire... just one shot each!"

Then he turned and strode purposefully after Gwion, the crowd drawing back to let them both pass.

Limestone... he must have heard about its hardening effects from the Romans. Mixed with brains... what would Felix the master craftsman have to say about *that* concoction, I wondered?

I was beginning to feel buoyant again. Although we were almost certainly doomed, my mind was drifting back into focus... perhaps it was the reassuring feel of my bow. I recalled the standing stones and the spirits of my forefathers. This ordeal was no more terrible than those my ancestors would have had to face. I felt sustained by their courage... eager to play my part in this deadly game.

But the look of remorse sweeping Ninian's face told a different story. He'd brought Plebius and me all this way from Novantes to face annihilation, and was powerless to intervene. I smiled and nodded encouragement to him, hoping to settle his mind.

"You...!" Tudwell was waving Plebius aside. "Stand back!"

Then, turning to me,

"And you...! Stay where you are... and be still!"

Eingel and Gwion had reached their firing position and were turning to face me. I could see Eingel hitching an arrow and preparing to take aim. Should I exhale to reduce my profile... sway a little to spoil his concentration? Or just observe... watch the trajectory... judge the fall, and be ready to move side-ways in a split second? But then Ninian's life depended upon me remaining motionless... be still, then. And vigilant!

Eingel elevated his bow. But surely he wasn't aiming high enough for a shot at that range... unless of course his weapon was a good deal more powerful than mine. The greater the power, the faster the arrow and the sooner it would reach me. A shorter flight time required a flatter trajectory. Yes... it all made sense... maybe his elevation was right after all! Another thought struck me... a faster arrow would give me less time to react!

Eingel's bow rang out. I froze... I'd lost sight of the arrow already! I searched for movement against the background of trees... nothing! I closed my eyes and waited... there came a low moan from the crowd... I'd neither seen nor heard the arrow fall. Enraged, Eingel struck out at the low-lying foliage with his bow.

Tudwell waved me aside and motioned for Plebius to take my place. Now it was Gwion who prepared to shoot.

"Good luck," I whispered.

Plebius remained passive and tight-lipped.

The delay was agonising... Gwion was taking careful aim. I heard a twang at the moment of release, followed by silence. There was a swish over my head, and another groan of disappointment from the crowd.

Tudwell's face reddened with exasperation.

"Give him an arrow!" he cried, pointing at me.

An arrow...? What arrow...? I responded without hesitation.

"I'll shoot with my *own* arrow!"

Tudwell frowned, and then nodded at someone in Eingel's gang. Suddenly my travelling pack and quiver were thrown to the ground in front of me.

My opportunity for revenge had come! The chance to vent my anger, to load my bow with all the hate I could muster for the odious Eingel, to exact satisfaction for all that wanton destruction and loss of life... for the pain inflicted on the young boy.

I stooped to select an arrow but caught sight of Ninian. There was something about his face... those expressive eyes. What had he told me? What had the Christ God tried to teach...? That forgiveness and mercy are the symbols of a dignified man. Down on one knee I took an arrow from my quiver. And then, instinctively, I searched my travelling pack for the target ball.

Again I glanced towards Ninian... he was already advancing towards me.

"I knew that I could rely on your good judgement, Gaelen."

He stooped forward and took the ball from my hand.

"Now..." he whispered. "We'll show them how much faith we have in God."

Straightening up, he turned to Tudwell.

"The Christian God has bestowed a wonderful gift on my friends, my lord... the gift of marksmanship. And if my friends can apply that skill to strike this ball from my hand, then I for one shall have good reason to praise Him!"

Tudwell looked perplexed as Ninian held the ball aloft and walked off towards Eingel and Gwion.

"Who's going to shoot first?" Plebius whispered.

I knew that Plebius would already have begun to address the challenge that Ninian had set us. I hadn't even started, and was beginning to have doubts.

"A hundred paces!" I gasped.

"Be single-minded!" Plebius urged. "Concentrate, Gaelen!"

The sound of his voice conveyed an inner determination to give the task his undivided attention, as if nothing else mattered. I felt totally unprepared in comparison to Plebius.

"You first," I said.

Eingel and Gwion were moving aside, leaving Ninian alone with my tiny ball resting in his out-stretched hand. Plebius took a stone from his pouch and held it up for everyone to see.

"This small stone was once intended for the head of Eingel!" he announced to the crowd. "...But now its name is 'Might Have Been'. For revenge, at first though sweet, is sour to God in the end!"

He placed the stone carefully into the saddle of the sling. Then he stood very still. I knew he'd be studying the target distance, the lie of the land... the strength and direction of the wind. At last he began to sweep the sling in slow circles around his head, first on a short string, but letting out more as the projectile gathered speed. I heard murmurings from the crowd, soon drowned by the sound of the sling as it reached its full length and began to produce that high pitched moan which signalled its readiness for release. I understood how Plebius's mind would be working... the greater the speed, the shorter the time of flight... and the less opportunity for crosswind to take effect.

Snap! Then a silence... it seemed like an age. And finally, that unmistakable sound... a dull and distant thud.

There was a cheer from the mob. I hardly dared to look, but braced myself and stole a glance towards where Ninian had been standing. He was still there... upright and motionless with the palm of his hand out-stretched. But the ball had disappeared!

My hunting instincts re-emerged as I too began to address the characteristics of the shot required for a flight of one hundred paces.

Whilst Ninian recovered the ball I closed my eyes. I felt a gentle breeze on my cheek; a cross wind, but short-lived. It faded away, and I opened my eyes to see that Ninian was again in position. The crowd was still making a lot of noise, but they seemed a world away to me. I locked the arrow to my bowstring, pulling back a little with my right hand to secure a firm union. Then I pointed the arrow at the ground, just a pace or two ahead, which is where I fixed my gaze. My brain had begun to rehearse the actions; my mind and body coming into alignment with that tiny leather target.

It was now very quiet, and I knew that every eye would be trained upon me. But I took my time. I would remain in this position until I felt ready to raise my bow. But suddenly everything felt right. Slowly... very slowly... up came the bow in my left hand, and back came the string in my right.

Focus...! Keep the left forearm straight as the right thumb comes under the chin. Check the horizontal line of the arrow; left a little... a little more. Here comes the pain, the muscular tremor, just as expected; no surprises this time. Now for the elevation; this was more difficult and would demand all my huntsman-like skills. Lay the arrowhead slightly above and to the right of Ninian's head. No...! Check again; quickly, before the awesome tension in the bow begins to spoil the aim... check again! There... a little higher for this range. Focus! Check the horizontal line again... does it still feel right? Yes, this must be it. Steady, then... hold still... remember to release the string quickly to avoid imparting a sideways movement to the arrow as the fingers detach them-selves... now!

I knew at that moment that I'd excelled myself. The arrow floated upwards, yawing a little from side to side before stabilizing and levelling off... then falling downwards into its descent. Once again a dull thud,

106

but this time the ball remained in Ninian's hand. The arrow must have passed through the ball, pinning itself to his palm! But no... he was smiling as he transferred the ball to his other hand and held it high in the air, the arrow still firmly in place.

At first I heard nothing as my mind slowly returned to the real world. Then I sensed the nearness of the mob... they were on the move and heading in my direction. My death was fast approaching. Please, Christ God, make it swift... after all this, I surely deserved a quick and merciful end.

Then they were upon me... I lowered my head to await the first blow. I felt myself being jostled... then hoisted up into the air... hauled onto the shoulders of fighting men, the noise deafening as I grappled with arms, hands, spears... anything to keep my balance. These were cries of jubilation... aroused by Ninian's bravery and Plebius's magnificent feat of marksmanship. There were glances for me as well, appreciative and complimentary. Running my eyes over the multitude of bobbing heads I caught sight of Plebius... he too had been borne aloft. And then Ninian, toppling and swaying as if he'd lost the power to steady himself. Close to him, I saw a smaller figure... the young boy seated astride the shoulders of a Pictish giant.

As we were paraded through the settlement I began to feel renewed in my mind, as if suddenly presented with a lifetime of fresh opportunities; and in my body, as the pains in my arms and shoulders had all but vanished.

And yet I had no right to this adulation. I hadn't asked for it; nor had I deserved it. There was a time when I'd have struck that ball from twice the distance, and without hesitation.

Worse still, my adoption by these Pictish warriors, however short-lived it may prove to be, had been at a price. Eingel and Gwion had suffered a grave humiliation and would now prove even more hostile. They'd failed ignominiously in the eyes of their king, and the whole community.

We'd almost arrived back at Tudwell's hut when I heard a familiar sound... the swish of an arrow passing close to my head. Or was it my imagination? That figure standing alone at the edge of the forest with a bow in his hand... was it Eingel? I couldn't be sure... but I longed for this pointless revelry to end!

"I congratulate you, man of rags!" Tudwell seemed pleased when at last we were set down at the foot of his balcony steps. "It's rare in my experience for prisoners to be greeted with such affection. But then my people have a high regard for notable accomplishments. Good shooting deserves praise."

"Such gifts are from God," replied Ninian. "But they are worthless in the hands of heartless men."

Tudwell's expression changed, and his face bore that melancholy expression again.

"Ah... you mean Eingel," he replied. "I know that Eingel isn't the crack shot he used to be. I once gave thanks to the gods for men like Eingel. Their skill in battle played no small part in unnerving the Roman army. But now..."

"But now..." interrupted Ninian, "not even the power of a great king can keep Eingel from his butchery and senseless killing!"

Tudwell seemed taken aback at Ninian's outspokenness. But then he appeared to relax a little, shrugging his shoulders and drawing a deep breath.

"Eingel is held in high esteem by my people," he replied decisively. "They respect him... and since I am for my people, then so will I."

"That's not how I see it," replied Ninian, motioning towards the crowd, now beginning to disperse. "The way they reacted to Eingel's failure as a marksman showed that they're resentful of him. A great king deserves a better ambassador, my lord."

"You're a clever man, to be sure," Tudwell smiled. "And I have a mind to set you free. But beware, man of rags! This land is dominated by cutthroats... wherever there's trouble there'll always be someone like Eingel."

"That child, my lord..." Ninian was peering up at the balcony. "Is she yours?"

A small girl, aged perhaps five or six, stood alone looking down at us from the top of the balcony steps. There was a profound sadness in her face.

"My daughter," said Tudwell. "She grieves for her mother and brother. They are sick, man of rags. I'd surrender my kingship to prevent it... but my wife and son are dying."

So *that* was it... that's what lay behind the king's morbid appearance!

"They say I'm a good healer," said Ninian. "Why not let me see them? If I can restore them to good health, I'll not ask for your kingship... just that you'd let me stay a while longer in Cadder."

Tudwell seemed pensive as he gazed up at his daughter. There was a long pause before he answered.

"Yes... examine them, if you will," he muttered, turning back to Ninian. "But tread carefully, man of rags! My wife and son are without equal!"

They mounted the steps together and entered Tudwell's hut. The girl followed on behind.

Plebius took a deep breath and exhaled noisily.

"When Ninian's finished, I'm going home," he announced firmly.

"He won't be in any mood to leave," I replied. "Cadder's important to his mission. We'll be here for ages... I might even have time to show you how to build a chapel, Plebius!"

The young orphan boy stood off to one side with the rope still fastened around his neck. I moved close, and knelt down beside him.

"My name is Gaelen." I began to loosen the rope. "What's yours?"

He remained speechless, head and eyes lowered towards the ground.

"Do you shoot?"

Still no answer...

"Did you see Plebius use his sling?"

The boy nodded.

"Plebius could teach you to shoot like that."

As he turned his tearstained face towards me I gained eye contact... and a shake of the head.

"No...? What, then...?"

He reached out, and with a look of determination gripped my bow. The boy had a score to settle.

"You're going to be a busy teacher," Plebius laughed, "...What with all that archery tuition, and showing me how to build in stone!"

"Plebius... Gaelen...!" Ninian was calling from the balcony. "Come quickly!"

As I entered Tudwell's hut the smell of sickness was almost overpowering. Ninian led us to the room where Tudwell's wife and son lay dying.

"Closer," urged Ninian, "... take a look."

"It's probably contagious!" complained Plebius, lingering at the doorway.

I took a deep breath, held it, and stepped forward to the bedside of Tudwell's son. He seemed younger than me... about fifteen, perhaps a little more. His face had a bluish tinge, sickly and wet with perspiration, and there were traces of vomit on the bed cover. His eyes, barely open, were staring vacantly at the ceiling, and he was foaming at the mouth. I glanced at his mother.

Her skin was the same; her breathing more laboured. I took another deep breath, and held it again.

"They've taken no food for days... only water." Tudwell sounded grave.

"Who gives them water?" asked Ninian. "Who looks after them?"

"My maidservant..."

There was a pause before Ninian spoke again.

"Well, Gaelen...?" His voice conveyed a sense of anticipation. "What do you make of all this?"

I glanced at Plebius, hoping for a clue. But he remained silent, his hand pressed firmly across his mouth.

"I don't know," I said. "It looks bad... that's all I can say."

Ninian turned back to Tudwell.

"Your misfortune is God's opportunity, my lord," he said. "With His help, your wife and son will live."

There was movement at the doorway. Plebius was being pushed aside... it was Eingel!

"Never trust a prisoner, my lord!" Eingel scowled. "If you listen to the man of rags, death will come quickly. I'll swear to it... two corpses before sunrise!"

"Leave us, Eingel," said Tudwell.

"But my lord...!" Eingel protested.

"Leave us, I say!" Tudwell exploded.

Eingel took a step backwards. He turned to me and I felt his eyes burning into mine. He'd missed his chance to kill me in a fair contest, but his demeanour showed that the game wasn't up. He turned swiftly away, and bumped heavily into Plebius as he careered out of the room.

Moments later a woman appeared holding a towel. Fair-haired, well groomed and very pretty, I saw immediately that she was a Celt... one of my own people.

"I... I wasn't warned of visitors," she stammered. "I must wash and refresh my mistress... and the prince Tostig." She looked frightened.

"It's alright, Maben," said Tudwell. "I'll call you when we've done."

She paused for a moment longer, and then she too was gone.

"Maben is my maidservant," said Tudwell.

His wife opened her eyes and groaned. Tudwell moved to the bedside and peered down at her.

"Treat her carefully, man of rags," he murmured. "There is no other woman with the capacity to lighten the darkest corners of my life."

"You can leave her safely with me, my lord." Ninian began ushering Tudwell towards the door. "Spend some time with the Christian God, and be assured that none who put their trust in Him shall be denied mercy."

The king hesitated, but Ninian remained firm... he was taking control of the sickroom. I watched as Tudwell left us... a deeply worried man.

"What can we do?" whispered Plebius, his voice filled with apprehension. "We're free to go Ninian. We could go now! But... but if these people die, then God knows what they'll do to us!"

The woman rolled onto her side and uttered a terrible retching sound.

"Then we shall have to work a miracle," replied Ninian calmly.

Plebius and I glanced at each other in disbelief.

"But we must be swift," he continued. "These people are being poisoned... hemlock probably... or mandrake. It doesn't matter which. What matters is that we induce vomiting, and then guard them closely over the next few days. Both of you... go down to the Clyde... bring salt water. Quickly! You'll be doing something to create a new servant for God... that's the whole purpose and nature of a miracle! And what a fish we shall catch... a Pictish king!"

Gathering up our water containers, Plebius and I raced through the settlement and rushed headlong into the forest. Plebius ran ahead, hollering and cheering as he leapt some fallen trees, darting from side to side to negotiate the narrow twisting path. Finally, as we charged down the final embankment, we both lost our footing, and I rolled over several times before coming to rest at the edge of the mighty river Clyde.

We could afford to be light-hearted now. Ninian was known to be accomplished in the art of healing after all his years of training in Rome. I was confident in my heart that he above all others would have the ability to save the lives of King Tudwell's wife and son.

CHAPTER 9

Winter, the season of frost and death, was drawing to a close. Leaving my tiny hut I breathed the cold morning air, gathering my resolve to face another day's work. Ninian and Plebius had been away since last autumn; leaving me to supervise the construction of Cadder's chapel, the first of its kind in Strathclyde. But problems kept piling up and progress was slow. Good limestone was difficult to find, torrential rain had turned the site into a mud bath, and my Pictish helpers were recalcitrant.

Yesterday, my workers had joined with the rest of the Cadder folk to celebrate Imbolc, the arrival of early spring. Imbolc was a Celtic festival, but these Picts had adopted it as an excuse for wanton promiscuity. My people would be making offerings to Brigid, the goddess of womanhood and of learning. What they'd have thought about Pictish behaviour during Imbolc I could hardly imagine. The Picts saw Imbolc as an opportunity for orgiastic rioting. Where were the Bards...? The sounds of the harp...? The poetry around the fire...? The youngsters whispering devotions to their sweethearts...? Last night the noise had been unbearable.

I'd wandered away from Cadder, far from all the drinking and debauchery, and found a quiet spot to study the stars. Perhaps Apolonia had been gazing upwards at that same moment. I'd thought of Kaylin too, for Imbolc was an opportunity to dwell on relationships... to plan new enterprises in the coming year... a time for maidens to make Bride dolls in honour of Brigid.

I was still alone now, as I made my way towards the building site.

Glancing into the forest I saw a faint colour in the treetops... new shoots beginning to sprout. Through a gap in the trees I caught sight of the Clyde, wide and majestic, its surface flat and calm save for a few gentle eddies stirred by the dense overhanging vegetation.

I stopped for a moment, struck by a notion of what Cadder might become after an inestimable number of years. These were a restless and vigorous people whose revelries would continue all night leaving them good for nothing but sleep in the morning. But they were adventurous sailors too, and made good use of the Clyde to reach the sea. I could imagine this place becoming a centre for boat building and for trade with distant lands; if only they could learn to moderate their drinking.

There was still no sign of my workers.

I started with an inspection of the site and saw that one of the chapel walls, now at shoulder height, had started to lean. I should have remembered my Novantes experience... Felix had dangled a stone to test each wall for uprightness at frequent intervals. Reluctantly I decided the wall would have to be demolished; I bent down to pick up my hammer.

"Why are you on your own, Gaelen?"

I looked up to see Tostig, King Tudwell's teenage son, staring down at me from the edge of the site. He looked well after his close encounter with death the previous summer. His recovery had inspired Tudwell to believe that the Christ God had intervened to save the lives of his wife and son. In my opinion it was Ninian who'd brought them back from the brink of death; plus the diet of pure goats' milk which he'd administered for much longer than both would have wished. The culprit who'd poisoned them hadn't been traced, and Ninian had chosen not to voice his views.

"Speculation is like a hawk amongst doves," he'd said. "...Better to keep it locked away."

"You look lonely," Tostig persisted.

"It's my fate," I sighed. "The days are short, the work is long, and your men folk have no patience to see it through. They probably left their brains in their drinking cups last night."

"I can help!" Tostig picked his way through the mud towards me.

"Alright... we'll start by knocking down this wall."

"But it's a *good* wall!"

"No... can't you see the lean? It has to come down now, or the whole building will fall. What would your mother say if you were inside and the roof fell on your head?"

I wondered about his mother. It was fortunate for us that she'd survived the poisoning. If she'd died, Tudwell's fury would have known no bounds... what a field day for Eingel!

"How is your mother... is she well?"

"She's fine. She said that you spend a lot of time on your own, Gaelen."

"Tell her I'm happier like that." I smiled. "When this is finished I'll be going home to my own family... mind your eyes!" I struck the top of the wall with the hammer and a large stone fell to the ground. "Make a neat pile... we'll be using the stones again!"

"I saw you teaching that orphan boy how to shoot," said Tostig, struggling to lift the stone.

He would be thinking about Callum, the Celtish child who'd witnessed the massacre of his father last summer. Although just seven years of age, he'd learned archery quickly.

"Callum...?" I replied. "Callum wanted to avenge the murder of his family. But now he's learning restraint, and good hunting skills... cover your eyes!" I struck with my hammer and another stone broke away.

"I asked my father if I could see you about some shooting practise."

"And what did he say?"

Tostig hesitated before answering dolefully.

"He didn't say you *couldn't* teach me."

"But what were his exact words?"

"He said that few archers reach old age." And then after a short pause, "...But I really *do* want to learn, Gaelen."

"Yes... I see you do. Eyes...!" Sparks flew as my hammer shattered a nodule of flint.

"Can I tell him you'll teach me, then?"

I looked at Tostig again. He was growing into a fine teenager and might one day inherit his father's king-ship.

I tried to imagine Tudwell's feelings. Having managed to overthrow the Romans, he'd embarked on an even greater challenge... that of encouraging his people to live peaceably. After capturing Cadder two summers ago they'd made progress in clearing large tracts of woodland; establishing grass areas for live-stock and space for cereal growing. But there was no controlling the greed of Pictish fighting men... plunderers and degenerate killers like Eingel. Especially not with Celtish lands in the south offering even richer prospects. Maybe Tudwell was grooming his young successor to adopt the role of a peacekeeper, and not to become a warmonger.

"What shall I say?" Tostig demanded.

"Tell your father that archery practice of itself creates no enemies... its war and hatred that bring the skill of marksmanship into bad repute. If he agrees with that, then I'll be happy to teach you."

Tostig beamed with pleasure.

"Where are your friends, Gaelen?"

"Ninian and Plebius...? They're somewhere in the north; over the Clyde, and beyond the Campsie Fells."

"Is that your home?"

"No. I live in the south... at a village called Fleet."

"Fleet...? Where exactly...?"

"Face the mid-day sun, walk until you fall into the sea; then you'll know you're there."

I lifted the hammer to strike another blow but saw Tostig looking past me. I turned to follow his gaze.

It was Eingel, staring down at me from the edge of the site, swaying as if still affected by last night's excesses. Unarmed and vulnerable, I began to back away. Besides, any closer and I'd be forced to breathe that aura of unpleasantness that always seemed to surround him.

Then I saw someone else strolling towards us.

Tostig took a few steps forward, and cried out, "Father...!"

Eingel spun round. On seeing the king approaching he coughed violently and spat on the ground. Then he skulked away.

"What's this...?" yelled Tudwell. He sounded annoyed. "What are you doing... making a *slave* of my son?"

"I *wanted* to help, father!" Tostig protested.

"Yes... yes I know." The disapproving scowl on Tudwell's face began to melt away. "But unhappily, your mother has been watching you wallowing like a

118

pig in the mud... a prince should know better!"

"Gaelen said he'd teach me archery, father!"

"Not without your permission, my lord," I added quickly.

"Archery...!" Tudwell frowned with disapproval, but then nodded and appeared to give way.

"I suppose shooting might be less ruinous to the boy's health; more rewarding than learning how to demolish stone walls, anyway. But I'll not have him make a fool of himself!"

"I could teach him how to hunt," I replied. "...There's much to learn about hunting, even before taking hold of a bow."

Tudwell seemed pleased.

"Well then...!" he cried. "Out of the mud Tostig... go and get cleaned up. The lessons will start today!" And then turning to me, "But first, you and I must speak!"

As Tostig sped away the king motioned for me to accompany him back to the settlement.

"A word with you", he said. "...About Maben."

"Maben, my lord...? Your maidservant...?"

"Ay, Maben... the Celt... a *splendid* creature." He glanced at me sideways. "She's young... and a good woman about the house. I spared her... on account of her prettiness."

"What happened to her family?"

"They fought well... and died bravely. But Maben..." He was shaking his head. "...By receiving that woman into my house I kindled a fire which can't so easily be put out. She's not one of us, Gaelen... she needs her own kind. When she's not on duty she stays in her room, grieving and pining like a lactating ewe that's lost its lambs."

We came to a stop and he put his hand on my shoulder, looking searchingly into my eyes.

"Have you considered taking a partner, Gaelen?"

"Ah...! No, my lord... I haven't!"

It was a lie... but how was he to know?

"Then you should," he grinned, "... and my wife thinks so too! Just imagine it, Gaelen... the three best things in life... hen's eggs, roast pig, and a good woman's praise!"

How could I disengage from this, without upsetting him?

"And the worst thing...?" I replied. "The worst thing might be a *bad* wife."

I felt my mouth drying up as Tudwell's face reddened. I'd been kept alive at his mercy since arriving here last summer. Now he was offering me the hand of his own maidservant, and I was about to cross him by appearing ungrateful.

"Besides, I..." Should I tell him about Kaylin and Apolonia? "I must collect my bow, my lord."

It was time for me to take my leave.

"I'll meet your son outside my hut when he's ready."

I scuttled away, not daring to look back.

*****

We moved slowly through the forest on a blanket of dead bracken and rotting leaves until we reached a small clearing. There, I brought my two young pupils to a halt.

The ravages of winter had uprooted many trees. Most had toppled to the ground, but some had lodged themselves against sturdier upright specimens. The colours were magnificent; shades of brown, gold and green, enriched by the bright spring sunshine and interspersed with sparkles of light reflected from beads of moisture which clung to every bough. This would be a good place to begin Tostig's training as a hunter.

"You see," I whispered, "... it's impossible to move without making a sound. So we have to advance carefully."

"Father told me I could use *his* bow!" Tostig spoke in a low voice, but his frustration was evident. "... Callum has a bow, and I'm older than he is!"

I'd forbidden Tostig to bring a bow, and I knew he'd be feeling sore about it.

"Here... try mine..." whispered Callum, holding out his tiny bow.

"Not long enough, Callum," I smiled, "He'll need one twice that size! Now, Callum... your task is to hunt for woodpigeon. We'll meet back here... and try not to lose any arrows!"

Crouching low, Callum moved off into the undergrowth. I turned to Tostig.

"See how Callum is learning to be stealthy? He knows how to recognise the nearness of his prey and to stalk it without revealing his presence. That's what you must learn to do, Tostig. And for that you don't need a bow."

I felt sorry for the boy, but it was important to enforce the basics of good hunting before trying to developing his shooting skills. That was how my father taught me. By the end of my early training the yearning to hold a bow had reached such a pitch that it created an enthusiasm for marksmanship which never left me. As I looked at Tostig I could almost feel his disappointment.

"When you can advance to within twenty paces of a deer, then I'll make you a bow that'll surpass all others. Now... be silent."

I breathed slowly and deeply, the smell of decaying bracken filling my senses.

"Springtime is good for learning," I whispered. "We can see far without lots of greenery getting in the way, and we don't have the rustling leaves to dampen the sounds. Now; what do you hear?"

Tostig lowered his head. Was he listening... or just moody and sullen?

"A bird... it sounds angry," he murmured.

"It is angry; we've trespassed into its territory. What else?"

"The wind... there...." He glanced up at the tree-tops.

"Good... now put those sounds out of your mind. What else?"

"A seagull..."

"Well done, Tostig; he's at the mouth of the Clyde, a very long way from here."

"And there's something moving... on the ground, over there!"

"A wood mouse, foraging," I whispered. "It's been a long winter. Now feel the wind on your face. From which direction is it blowing?"

"From over there, I think." He pointed vaguely towards the densest part of the forest.

"And that's where most of your hunting will be done. You'll learn to recognize the scent of the different creatures borne on the wind; first the wild boar, then the deer. And if you get really good then the smaller animals... weasel, hedgehog and squirrel. But you'll need to develop your senses."

"How will I know it's a deer?

"Ah... that's the greatest challenge. The deer treads lightly... and moves very little unless disturbed. Not even the birds will betray its presence. But a deer will give itself away, Tostig. Listen for it brushing against a leaf, the gentle nudge of a twig... and not just once, but again and again from the same direction. And then

122

there's the scent. Believe me... you'll know when you're creeping up on a deer."

Once again I inhaled deeply. I hadn't been sure about it at first, but now I felt confident that something had moved to within stalking range.

"Stay here Tostig... see if you can identify what I'm after. I'll be back very soon."

Locking an arrow to my bowstring I moved cautiously, still unsure about what lay ahead. The scent was unfamiliar; clearly it was no ordinary creature of the forest. I advanced stealthily and then knelt, lowering my head, and racking my brain for an explanation.

Then I heard it... the sudden slap of a taught string followed by the swish of an arrow. I froze... a cry of pain... Tostig!

In a flash my mind was transformed from a state of quiet vigilance to one of frenzied alarm. I found myself sprinting and crashing through the under-growth... back to where I'd left him. And then I shuddered to a halt... Tostig lay crumpled on the ground!

Even now I dared to believe it might be a game; please, Christ God, let this be a joke... a plot contrived between Tostig and Callum to catch me out. But no... the shaft was firmly lodged in the front of his neck. I fell to my knees, lifted my face to the sky and cried out.

"Callum...!"

A flock of ravens took flight as my voice echoed through the forest.

I'd trusted Callum to bear no malice... to harbour no grudge... to know that revenge can never mend a broken heart. I looked down again at the face of Cadder's lifeless prince... at the eyes of Tudwell's son, still open, blank and unmoving. I shivered with foreboding.

But... that arrow... it was long! I'd made Callum's arrows very short! And those feathers... white goose wing, with sparrow-gut binding. The arrow belonged to me! I looked into Tostig's face and shuddered again... his eyes were staring up into mine! The fury of every Pictish god was about to descend on me!

"Gaelen," he said weakly. "...Am I going to die?"

"No... not before me." I tried to sound reassuring.

I felt round to the back of his neck and breathed a sigh of relief... I could feel the barb. The shaft had entered at the side of his neck, protruding behind and missing his windpipe and major arteries. There was surprisingly little bleeding. With the barb removed, perhaps the shaft could be drawn out without causing further injury. But I'd need help; I must get him back to the settlement.

"Gaelen...!" someone cried out.

I turned to see Callum gasping for breath. He'd come up behind me.

"Gaelen..." he spluttered, "I heard you calling. I came as quickly as..."

Still panting, Callum's voice faded away as he looked down at Tostig.

I held out my bow towards Callum.

"Here... take it, Callum!"

Then I eased my arm under Tostig's shoulders, the other under his legs, and lifted him gently.

"Rest your head on my shoulder," I murmured, "... you're going home."

We moved off, the long shaft pointing skywards, its feathers swaying and trembling. I kept a rapid pace whilst trying to avoid jarring the wound. I looked down for signs of further haemorrhaging; blood around the mouth would spell the end... but there was none.

"Gaelen...," sobbed Callum from behind, "it's not my arrow... I didn't shoot him, Gaelen."

I was in no mood to respond. I would try to work it out later.

"What... what are you going to do, Gaelen?" Callum sounded petrified with fear.

I glanced back and saw him struggling to keep up. There was a crash as he stumbled, recovered, and raced forward again to close the gap between us.

"Never mind," I gasped, "... let's just get back!"

At last, and close to exhaustion, I broke free of the forest and staggered towards the centre of Cadder. We were seen immediately. At first there were muted sounds of astonishment, but not for long. By the time we'd reached Tudwell's hut, the noise of the crowd was almost deafening. The people closed in, their looks charged with hostility.

I sank to my knees and lowered Tostig to the ground. Then, sapped of all energy, I toppled forwards onto my hands to make a protective arch over him, letting my head flop.

The noise subsided, and I heard someone descending rapidly from the balcony steps. I raised my head slowly and saw Tudwell's leather boots, then his red cloak, and finally, at the limit of my upward gaze, the look of astonishment on his face as he towered over me. He appeared to be struggling with a torrent of emotions, but his loss of composure was brief.

"Surgeon!" he yelled, and the people took up the cry.

"Bring the surgeon...! Get Semias...! Find Semias, the surgeon...!"

After a few moments the crowd parted and a man burst into the open. He rushed towards us. In another moment I felt myself dragged off to one side. As I looked again, the surgeon was already down on his knees at work on Tostig's wound. I heard a snap, followed by a shrill scream. The bloody shaft was withdrawn and passed to Tudwell.

Another man swaggered forward... it was Eingel, his face flushed with self importance.

"That arrow, my lord," Eingel ranted, "...It belongs to the cringing chicken!" He was pointing at me. "Look at the feathers in his quiver... goose wing... just like the ones on the shaft in your hand!"

"The wound must be treated... and quickly!" yelled the surgeon, peering closely at Tostig's neck.

Tudwell seemed reluctant to shift his threatening gaze away from me, but then turned swiftly and stooped beside his surgeon to inspect Tostig's wound.

A woman called from the balcony, clearly distressed.

"Tell me!" she cried. "I have to know... is he badly hurt?" It was Tudwell's wife, her face pale and ghost-like.

The king looked up, shook his head, and motioned for Tostig to be borne away for treatment. Then, turning his attention back to me, he came closer. I staggered to my feet... the look of rage in Tudwell's face was real, but I must appear dignified.

"And to think I once thought highly of you." He spoke quietly, his voice trembling.

Then he turned to Eingel and gave full vent to his fury.

"You know what to do!" Tudwell roared. "Kill him...!"

"Willingly, my lord...!"

"But... but I didn't shoot him!" I stammered. My voice sounded hoarse, my mouth parched. "I'm innocent of all this!"

Eingel was closing fast, wheezing with excitement.

126

"Slow sport, my lord...?" He was drawing his short sword. "Or clean and brisk...?"

Before Tudwell could reply, the strained silence was broken by the frenzied cry of a distraught woman.

"No...! No...! This is unjust!"

Tudwell spun round to face the balcony. The woman continued, sobbing.

"Don't you see, my lord? Eingel forced me to poison your wife... and your son. Eingel threatened me."

I glanced up at the woman. It was Maben, Tudwell's maidservant.

"Eingel wanted to take over your kingship," she cried. "He tortured me. I had to keep silent; he wanted me to murder your wife and son, and then you...!"

"She lies...!" boomed Eingel, shaking his sword at her. "Don't believe her, my lord!"

My eyes were drawn to the quiver around Eingel's waist; a white-feathered arrow stood out amongst several other drab specimens. Goose wing... it was mine! This was theft! Eingel must have stolen two of my arrows. He'd shot one at Tostig, and had kept one in reserve... just in case. But he'd blundered!

I glanced back at Tudwell. His gaze was shifting from the blood-smeared shaft in his hands to the arrow in Eingel's quiver... awakening to the realization he'd been tricked. I was about to speak, but was cut short.

"Take him!" cried Tudwell, reaching out towards Eingel.

But the stunned crowd reacted too late. With his sword raised high, Eingel turned on his heels and rushed headlong into their midst, slashing and cleaving as he fled. I saw blood and heard a yelp of pain as a severed hand fell to the ground. Some of the mob tried to corner him, but his skill and determination with the sword kept them back. Eventually they gave way. A few brave men chased after him; I saw his head through the crowd darting this way and that in his desperation to evade them. Then he was gone.

Eingel had escaped, vanishing swiftly into the dense forest.

CHAPTER 10

Surrounded on all sides by the Galloway hills, I stood beside a narrow stretch of inland water known locally as Loch Trool. I gazed across the loch's placid surface, and then upwards at the steep ridge on the other side. Just below its rocky summit, a sweep of darkened heather traced the site of last autumn's purple bloom, now spent. My eyes moved lower, taking in the fresh green bracken which clung to the middle slopes, and lower still to the dense forest of deciduous trees reaching down to the shoreline.

Then my gaze rested on the loch itself, flat calm with the lofty landscape on the farther side mirrored on its surface. But the reflection wasn't quite perfect... fish were rising and breaking the surface in their constant hunt for food. I could imagine the scene underwater; the battle for survival between the hungry brown-speckled trout and the Mayfly nymph struggling upwards from the muddy depths to be free of its natal origins. A circular ripple... another fly sucked to its death.

"Gaelen...!" Someone called.

I turned. Over my shoulder I saw Callum, waist high in the bracken, running down the steep slope to join me.

"Gaelen...!"

He came to a stop beside me, gasping for breath.

"Ninian said we can stay here tonight," he panted. "It's Maben... she's too tired to go on."

Poor Maben, I thought. She was unused to travelling, and hadn't realized how arduous the journey south was going to be.

She'd begged King Tudwell for permission to adopt Callum, and to allow them both to return with us to Galloway. Tudwell had been reluctant to let them go... especially Maben. But Ninian had intervened on their behalf, and the king had consented in the end.

Maben and Callum had lost their entire families to Pictish brutality, and I'd little doubt that the murderous Eingel was at the heart of their misfortunes. Ninian had promised them both a warm welcome... a lasting home in his father's village. And we were nearly there. Tomorrow, they would be safely established in Novantes.

"Maben has every right to rest," I said. "Ninian walks quickly and expects everyone else to keep up. But you're surviving it well, Callum."

He was looking around inquisitively.

"Yes... but why are you down here, Gaelen?"

"Why? Sometimes I like to be on my own... that's why." I gazed back over the loch. "I was thinking about catching some fish; wouldn't that be a surprise for Ninian and Plebius?"

Callum shook his head.

"I can't catch fish... I don't know how."

"Can't catch fish...?" I smiled. "So what's that slung over your shoulder?"

"This...?" He reached up and touched his bow.

"Yes... *that*. Come on... let's get our legs wet."

I stepped into the cold water and waded out until it covered my knees. Callum followed up to his thighs. He held his bow at the ready, flat across the surface of the water to keep it dry.

"The fish are blind with greed," I whispered. "...See how close they come."

A large trout swept in front of us, its dorsal fin leaving a wake on the surface.

"Try a shot, Callum."

He raised his bow, and waited... but not for long. Another good sized fish appeared a short distance ahead. His arrow tore into the water, disappeared briefly, and then bobbed to the surface like a dead twig.

"But... I aimed straight towards it!" he exclaimed with a look of disbelief.

"Yes," I laughed, "But that's no way to shoot through water. A submerged target always appears shallower than it really is. You'll have to aim *underneath* the fish... try again."

It was some time before another trout was tempted to glide within range. As it rose to engage a fly, a flash of white and a sharp intake of air betrayed the snap of its mouth. At that same instant, Callum released his arrow. It plunged downwards and came to a sudden stop, even before the feathers had touched the water. The shaft trembled briefly, and was then motionless... a sizeable fish had been impaled and killed cleanly. Callum gave a cry of joy.

"Shh...!" That's just the first," I whispered. "If you're quiet, there'll be more."

Callum claimed another, and then I shot three. We'd caught five altogether; one for each of our party. We clambered back up the slope to where the others were resting in the shade.

Maben appeared to be asleep. Callum raced towards her, a trout raised up in each of his hands, hooked by his fingers under the gills.

"Maben... look! I caught them!"

She opened her eyes, sat up and shrieked.

131

"Ha...!" Plebius teased. "That's very funny, Maben... you manage to live with the barbarians for three long years, cooking for them, waiting on their chief and putting up with all their bad habits... but you still can't stand the sight of two little fish!"

"I can so!" she protested, scrambling to her feet. "I was startled, that's all! Go and find some kindling... I'll show you how to cook!"

Maben took the catch from Callum's outstretched hands.

"They're lovely," she continued. "Come with me, Callum... we'll find some herbs to make them taste really nice."

Maben, Callum and Plebius moved off, leaving me alone with Ninian. He was sitting against the trunk of an old oak, the sacred tree of our people.

I'd never felt it necessary to engage in small-talk with Ninian. I felt it beneath him. He had the power to enthral, and if by chance he should choose to speak, then I knew I would forget all time. We sat gazing out across the loch, each with our own thoughts.

I began to dwell on a dilemma which had troubled me since leaving Cadder many days ago. Tomorrow I would be faced with a decision; perhaps the most difficult of my life. Should I part company with my friends, and head for my own home by the Fleet River? Or should I stay with them; stroll into Novantes and suffer the anguish of seeing Plebius reunited with Apolonia?

He'd spent a lot of time with her before leaving Novantes last year. And how could I forget that Ninian himself had made a point of telling me of Plebius's fondness for Apolonia? But if she was so attached to Plebius, what should I think of her behaviour towards me... that fiery moment of passion on the eve of our parting? How could she have allowed herself to indulge in all that emotion, and leave me with such a sense of longing?

I couldn't fathom it out. But I was inclined to think that I must give way honourably... return to Fleet, and leave Plebius to what was rightfully his.

I glanced at Ninian. He too seemed deep in thought. Dare I tell him of my predicament? He'd been pleased with the way I'd built the chapel at Cadder almost single-handed. Apart from the want of a limestone wash, it might have compared favourably with Felix's efforts in Novantes. Yes... I'd served Ninian well. But how would he respond to the idea of his sister being pursued by a lowly hunter? It might end our fellowship... could I bear that?

Ever since we'd first met, when I was just ten, I'd viewed Ninian as an outstanding individual. I'd remembered his example ever since that time, even though he'd gone away to Rome. I'd thought about him a great deal whilst sitting beside the standing stones, the hallowed grave of my forefathers, and pondered about the meaning of life. And then, during this past year, we'd been through so much together.

He turned and caught me looking at him... those blue eyes seeming to scan the deepest recesses of my soul.

"Your mission, Ninian... It's nearly over."

"Ah...you think so?" His voice sounded wistful and trancelike, as if he'd scarcely withdrawn from a deeply hypnotic experience in the otherworld... that place he called heaven, the Kingdom of God.

"Not for a long time yet, Gaelen... not until the passing of a millennia or two. Perhaps then we might begin reap the harvest of my mission."

"Two millennia...!" I exclaimed. "That's two thousand years, isn't it?"

I'd often tried to visualize what it would be like that

far in the future, but had lacked imagination and insight.

"Two thousand years," Ninian smiled. "But the peace of God reaches out much further than that, Gaelen. Two thousand years is as a single day with God... and a day is as two thousand years."

"But... you can't live that long... nobody can!"

"No... you're right," Ninian chuckled to himself. "But I pray that my soul will survive, Gaelen. I'd like to think that I could do something useful in two thousand years from now. There's certain to be some poor fellow needing support and guidance; someone feeling alienated by his society... muddled and worn down by the chaos of his time." He was looking at me intently. "There'll be a place for you too, Gaelen. But I'm not sure that God will so readily accept you... not with that look of torment on your face!"

"Torment...?" I swallowed hard. "It's not really. It's just that I have to think about tomorrow... which way to go; Novantes, or back to Fleet."

"Which way to go...?" Ninian sounded surprised. "If you mean what I think you mean, then there's only one path for you, Gaelen... why, it's as clear as crystal!"

So he knew everything! I was a sinner, unworthy of his company and a disappointment to the Christ God. Ninian might even banish me from Novantes for daring to think I could ask his sister to marry me. There was a pause before he continued.

"Plebius came to speak with me in private yesterday."

"Plebius...?" I muttered.

A cold wave of despair welled up inside me.

"Yes, Plebius... and why not...? The poor man was at his wits end... he came to seek my advice."

Plebius's mind in turmoil...? Was that possible?

He'd always appeared so calm. Had he been worrying about my feelings, just as I'd been concerned for his? That must be it! He'd sought Ninian's advice on how to persuade me to return to Fleet! I took a deep breath and prepared myself for what was to come... reprimand? Then expulsion...?

"It seems," Ninian continued, "that Plebius's problems began shortly after he and I returned from our mission north of Cadder."

Casting my mind back, I recalled the look of relief on Plebius's face as he walked into Cadder, having being away for several months.

"But Plebius was happy to return!"

"He was," Ninian continued, "until Tudwell took him aside and lectured him at some length about the virtues of marriage! Tudwell wanted to find a husband for Maben, and Plebius seemed the ideal choice. Tudwell had always felt guilty about the way her family had been annihilated, leaving her lonely and robbed of the company of her kinsfolk. The king has proved a clever matchmaker, Gaelen... Plebius has harboured a genuine fondness for the fair Maben ever since!"

"But... but, Apolonia!" I stammered.

"Apolonia...? Ah, yes... the root cause of Plebius's problems! It's true, Gaelen... Plebius has always been very fond of my sister. And of course he worried a great deal about what Apolonia would say when she discovered his feelings for Maben."

"And... and what did you say to Plebius?"

"Only that I thought it unwise for him to make up his mind on the basis of my poor counsel. But I assured him that Apolonia has a strong instinct for survival... and that I was firmly of the opinion that my sister had already won the heart of another young man."

He turned to gaze over the loch and I felt my anxieties slipping away.

"The young hunter smiles again," said Ninian thoughtfully, his eyes still resting on the distant shore. "...I can't imagine why."

*****

"What's that?" Maben had come to an abrupt halt, and was pointing ahead.

"It's the chapel!" cried Plebius.

Moving to her side, he took Maben by the hand.

"Yes," said Ninian, glancing at me. "And let's remember who we have to thank for it."

Ninian must have felt proud of the white chapel of Novantes, sparkling like a pearl amongst the rolling hills of the Machars. But in truth it was the creation of his builders, Felix and Marcus, not mine. It shone like a beacon, and our progress towards it was very rapid in the final stages of our long journey.

Somehow, the people of Novantes must have been forewarned of our imminent arrival; a cheering mass had gathered even before we set foot inside the settlement.

Brothers John and Stephen strode out in front of the crowd, followed by Felix and Marcus. And then Fabian, the small stout scribe struggling to keep up with them.

The crowd advanced to greet us and Ninian quickly disappeared from my view, engulfed in a wave of jubilation.

"Maben... Callum...!" I cried out in vain. I was already cut off from them, the sound of my voice lost in the clamour and excitement which had overtaken us.

I scanned the crowd for Plebius but he too had been

consumed in the free-for-all.

Now separated from my friends, I pushed myself away from the core, eager to be free of all the noise and commotion. I felt myself jostled and elbowed as I struggled outwards towards the fringe.

Then I looked back, searching for the one who'd occupied my thoughts day and night since leaving this place a year ago. She must be here... wouldn't she have come to see me? Once again I scanned the sea of waving arms, my heart beating faster as a sense of desperation grew inside me... had Plebius found her after all?

Only then did it occur to me... I was a fool to think she'd be here! Apolonia had grace and refinement; she wouldn't want to be swept up in all this noise and commotion. I turned towards the centre of the village and ran headlong for her father's home.

The settlement was deserted, just as it was a year ago when I'd first arrived from Fleet in the hope of seeing Ninian. It seemed like only yesterday. My advance had been slow and wary then; but now it was different. I felt myself racing like a wild and frantic deer, scattering the chickens in all directions in my haste to be close to her.

Coming at last to the foot of her father's balcony, I stopped to catch my breath... my lungs seemed ready to burst. I fought desperately against the temptation to rush up those steps; I must seek composure... appear calm.

Lifting my travelling pack off one shoulder, I let it fall to the ground. Slowly, some semblance of self control began to return. Then, with even slower deliberation, I slid my bow from the other shoulder and bent down to rest it beside my pack. I looked up at the balcony and felt myself moving forward, my mind numb as if suspended in time.

As I climbed I heard the rush of blood coursing through my brain. And there was something else; the sound of music... Apolonia's mother, Drusilla, would be playing her harp. For a moment I stood on the balcony, listening. And then the door swung slowly open.

She seemed exactly as I'd left her... her face pale and thin... her mouth expressive and sensitive... those loving eyes... and that long grey dress, drawn-in at the waist by a leather band. We stood in silence for a few moments. And then she spoke.

"You came back...," she smiled. "My hunter has returned home... from the hills."

I moved forward, gathering her into my arms and burying my head in her long dark hair. What was the point of trying to hide my tears? My whole body throbbed uncontrollably, and she'd know full well that I was crying.

I drew back a little, peering into her eyes... moist and loving.

I was about to speak... to say how much I'd missed her, but stopped short. The harmonious tones from Drusilla's harp had been overtaken by another sound... babbling and infant-like. I glanced back at Apolonia.

"I heard something," I said. "It sounded like..."

Drusilla appeared at the doorway... she was cradling a baby. I looked back into Apolonia's face.

"Welcome home, Gaelen," she beamed. "Welcome home... to your new son!"

I moved slowly away from Apolonia's embrace and approached Drusilla. I took the child, cradled him, and looked down at his sparkling blue eyes; those exquisite little hands, uncoordinated and jerking aimlessly as if uncertain of how to touch me. I felt the warmth of his presence, and breathed that scent which is unmatched by any but the smallest of babes.

"Don't be deceived," said Drusilla. "He's not always so calm."

Stretching out my arms, I raised him high above my head. He looked down at me, frowning and squinting.

"Have you named him?" I asked, glancing sideways at Apolonia. Her cheeks were flushed.

"No... of course not," she smiled. "Would I deny you the right to name your own child? I've been waiting for you to return."

I looked up at my tiny son. Should I name him after Ninian? No... it wouldn't be fitting... so few are truly unique among men.

"Plebius, then...!"

"Plebius...? A Roman name...?" Apolonia sounded doubtful. "What's wrong with a good Celtic name? Why not Padraic... the *nobly born*...?"

"So you *have* been thinking about it!" I laughed.

"No, it doesn't matter. If you prefer the name Plebius..."

"There's none braver than Plebius," I said.

I heard someone racing up the steps towards the balcony, and spun round. It was Apolonia's father, Chief Nechtan, his towering frame outlined against the dazzling sunlight shining through the doorway. He approached me, breathing heavily... his expression grim.

I froze with panic. I'd entered the sacred bond of parenthood with his treasured daughter... Ninian's sister... and had done so without seeking Nechtan's consent. How could I explain to Nechtan that nothing, absolutely nothing, would keep me away from Apolonia and our baby son?

I must be ready with my defence... I would protest that Apolonia was innocent of all this... that I'd taken advantage of her frailty at a weak moment. I'd heap the blame upon myself. But I wouldn't allow Nechtan to divide us, or to stigmatize the love I felt for his cherished daughter.

"Gaelen," he said gravely. "I've some bad news for you... prepare yourself."

"Bad news...?" I murmured.

Instinctively, I turned back towards Apolonia. The bloom in her cheeks had vanished. She came close and gently took the baby from my arms.

"It's your father's village," Nechtan continued. "They've been attacked!"

He was still talking, but the words seemed meaningless; distorted and almost drowned out by the loud humming in my ears. Then I caught a snippet of what he was saying...

"A messenger sailed directly from the scene... the raid was from inland."

There were more footsteps... Plebius!

"Gaelen...!" Plebius exclaimed.

It was all he could say, but his look was enough to reveal his sense of outrage.

"I must gather my forces!" said Nechtan, glancing anxiously at Drusilla. "We could be under attack ourselves within a day or two."

He turned to face me.

"Gaelen, the Roman garrison at Rispain has been disbanded... we're completely alone now. I must concentrate my efforts on defending Novantes. I wish it could be otherwise, but as things stand I dare not commit my forces to a retaliatory strike at Fleet."

I turned to Plebius, and knew he must be thinking like me.

"I have to go back," I said. "I have to go back and help my family... my people."

But I'd opened my mouth without thinking! How could I even think of leaving Apolonia?

"I'm coming with you!" Plebius sounded

140

determined.

"I'll give you a boat," said Nechtan, "... and one of my best sailors. He'll get you across the bay and up the Fleet River. The wind's set fair, but very strong... you'd better be prepared for a rough crossing!"

He turned away and rushed out of the room.

Apolonia's eyes were filling with tears as she handed our baby to Drusilla. Then she moved towards me and I drew her close. I wanted her to feel the fire that raged within me; that overwhelming sense of horror for the terrors which may have befallen my family. I wanted her to understand my anxiety and apprehension at the awful prospect of having to leave her.

Our embrace slackened... I pulled away slowly until only our hands remained clasped.

"Remember, Gaelen," she said softly, "I'm always with you... whatever happens."

Her fingers slid away, and we parted.

I descended the steps and found Plebius waiting for me. I lifted my dusty travelling pack and bow, threw them both over my shoulder, and then cast one final look behind.

I knew I would cherish the sight forever... that vision of Apolonia holding our little boy... a moment of unsurpassed intimacy.

I felt Plebius's comforting arm around me as we set out for the tiny harbour at the Isle of Novantes.

CHAPTER 11

Peering out from under my blanket I saw Plebius
standing close to the bow as if willing the boat to go
faster. I was cowering in the stern, clutching a
mooring line, and feeling sick in my stomach.

Our helmsman had described this as a following
sea... the best for making good speed. But its ferocity
devastated my senses. As each huge wave passed
under the stern I found myself lifted high into the air,
gazing down upon Plebius as if from the top of a hill.
And then, as the powerful swell moved forward, I saw
him thrust upwards to become silhouetted against the
dark grey sky. I admired his courage. There were just
the three of us on board, and it would have been
difficult to save him had he gone over the side.

"Not long now, master Gaelen!"

I exchanged glances with the helmsman, his rugged
face lined with the evidence of a lifetime on the high
seas. He stood with both hands grasping the tiller, and
I could tell from his confident smile that he was well
accustomed to these conditions.

"Lift yourself up," he yelled, "and you'll see the
hills of Fleet!"

"And be washed overboard," I groaned.

I was content to stay under my blanket. I didn't
even want to think about what we'd find on our
arrival... I just wanted to be there, and quickly.

The helmsman glanced away and scanned the horizon. Maybe he was worried about being spotted and intercepted by the raiders. It seemed unlikely; according to Chief Nechtan they'd come from inland, not from the sea.

I began to focus on the situation; trying to imagine the pressures on my family.

Ossian, my brother, would be full of ideas, but he was timorous and ineffectual when it came to getting things done... he couldn't even *lift* an axe, let alone run with it.

Mother would be a pillar of strength, of course. She'd be doing her best to control my father's impulsiveness, and trying to prevent a hasty and ill-conceived campaign of revenge.

And then I thought of Kaylin. Not for the first time I'd drawn comfort from her Bride doll, still safe inside my jacket. I thought about our mad dash through the Beltane fire just moments before we'd parted company. Even now I could see her glowing cheeks... her tearful smile mingling with the smoke and ash, and her impassioned face flushed by the heat of the flames. I wanted her to know that I was thinking of her, and longed to be assured that she was safe.

I threw off my blanket, grasped the side of the boat, and levered myself up. Then, clinging firmly to a rough wooden safety barrier, I looked down into the black unwelcoming sea... my greatest dread. What had the Druid warned my mother after my little brother was drowned all those years ago?

"The sea likes to be visited from time to time, but when tempestuous it's better to fish for seaweed than risk losing a son."

Now more than ever I could appreciate the sense of what he was trying to say... keep inshore, and avoid the ocean at all costs!

I forced myself to look farther into the water... below the chaotic churning of those awesome waves. An image began to form, shimmering and indistinct at first, but coalescing into a recognizable likeness. It was a face... pale, tranquil and smiling; my younger brother! He was looking up at me!

And then, as the image faded, another appeared; the bushy head of an animal. Balor! My one-eyed hound... Balor the sea god! I should have known he wouldn't abandon me.

The two spirits I held most dear had risen from their blissful sleep in the otherworld, singling me out for their encouragement and protection. I began to recover my nerve and glanced towards the Fleet estuary. Somewhere in those hills, high above the tree line, lay the sacred grave of my forefathers.

"Patience, master Gaelen!"

I felt the helmsman's hand on my shoulder. I'd been leaning out too far and perilously close to the water. He drew me back. And then, easing on the tiller, he turned us gently into the lee of the rising ground. The sea was calmer here, and our speed slowed to little more than a walking pace.

"Look...!" cried Plebius. "Isn't that where your home is?"

He was pointing towards the Fleet River. A pall of smoke rose slowly from behind some trees. Then, caught by the wind, it was being drawn into long streaks and blown further up the river valley. Nothing out of the ordinary... smoke was often to be seen rising over my village. Perhaps they were all well... maybe the attack had been repulsed... or maybe it had never happened?

Glancing into the hills again, I caught sight of the standing stones. I'd climbed to that spot so many times, even as a child. How often had I stood on that mound of grass looking out across the Solway without realising that one day I'd be tossed like a leaf on this same stretch of water? And how often had I sat beside the stones trying to fathom the purpose of my life, never imagining that I was destined to accompany a great man on his quest to bring peace and order in the land of the Picts?

"I can't take you much further, boys!" The helmsman shifted his gaze from one bank to the other. "If I run into trouble here, I'll never get the boat around!"

"Let us off!" yelled Plebius. "Gaelen... is it far from here?"

That smoke... surely it was thicker than usual.

"Gaelen...!"

"What...?" I was startled... jolted back to reality like a nervous deer caught unawares. "No..." I yelled. "It's not far!" I pointed to a spot on the riverbank I knew would give a quick route to my village. "It'll best if we land over there!"

"Come on, then!" Plebius motioned for the boat to go faster. "We can run faster than this!"

Folding my blanket, I turned to face the helmsman.

"I haven't much to offer," I said, holding out the bundle. "Would you accept this as payment?"

"Ay... that I would, master Gaelen." He looked very sombre. "Away with you then; and give my respects to Chief Latinus."

I laid the blanket at his feet, slung my bow and travelling pack across my shoulder, and moved forward to join Plebius. The boat passed smoothly alongside the grassy bank, and we leapt ashore.

Plebius ran ahead at a frantic speed, and I soon lost sight of him; sheer exhaustion had begun to slow me down.

We'd set off from Loch Trool before sunrise to cover the final stretch of our journey from Cadder to

Novantes. Ninian had forced the pace, and we'd arrived in Novantes before noon. Even now I could feel that sense of excitement, being reunited with Apolonia, learning of my fatherhood, and cradling our baby. And then I'd suffered that deep wounding pain... my spirits crushed by the news of an assault on Fleet, and the agony of being parted from my cherished family. What would I have done without Plebius? With my mind still reeling from the terrible shock, he'd escorted me down to the Isle of Novantes where we'd boarded the fishing boat... we'd endured a dangerous sea crossing. And now, having been on the move all day, I was beginning to weaken.

The track was narrow and overhung with brambles tearing at my arms and legs. Reaching a patch of open ground, I paused to glance back across the sea.

It was a breathtaking scene. The forests and pasturelands of the Machars were bathed in sunbeams all radiating from a common point which lay hidden behind the clouds. Tonight, instead of dipping his fiery body into the sea, the sun god Belanus would choose to leave the world through the gates of Novantes. The view contrasted dramatically with the massive sheet of black cloud which hovered above my head like an impenetrable mantle. I set off again, and was soon amongst the trees which bordered our settlement.

In a few moments I'd be home! My parents would be impatient to hear about where I'd been in the past year. I'd tell Ossian about my devotion to Apolonia; that I'd sealed the union forever with a lovechild.

And what would I say to Kaylin? She'd feel hurt about my newfound attachment, and I was worried about that. I'd tell her the truth... that she would always be important to me... more than a foster sister. I'd explain that neither the hostile judgement of our

Druid, nor the merciless power of the sea, could suppress the love I'd always feel for her. I felt a surge of exhilaration, and careered ahead with renewed energy.

Emerging at last into the open I stopped dead in my tracks. I knew how things *should* be... the arrangement of our huts, my family home at the centre, the people going about their daily duties... and the children running to greet me. But this was just a barren wasteland! Where had it all gone? There had to be a sensible explanation; they must have bundled everything together and moved out, leaving nothing but a few smouldering piles of unwanted rubbish.

I saw someone moving. It was Plebius. He'd gone to inspect the site, and was starting back towards me. I moved forward.

"Stay away!" he called. "There's nothing you can do, Gaelen!" I continued towards him. "Stop!" he yelled, stretching out his arms to bar my way.

"Let me go!" I cried, trying to move around him. But Plebius was determined to block me. He looked spent... hopeless.

"Don't go," he pleaded. "It's no use, Gaelen. They're... they're all dead."

"No...!" I made another attempt to slip past, refusing to believe what I'd heard him say. "They've moved away... that's all... they've gone somewhere else!"

"You're wrong, Gaelen! I saw them... just a moment ago!" He was panting heavily, almost sobbing. "Believe me, a quick look... that was enough." He held me firmly by the arms, his eyes filling with tears. "I'm sorry, Gaelen... there's nobody left alive... it's just a mess. It's even worse than..."

The sound of his voice faded until I could hear nothing but the pounding of my heart and the roar of blood surging through my brain.

So... that was it? I'd been looking forward with such hope, but all the time I'd been deluding myself. The outline of Plebius's face began to blur, and the whole world misted over. I let my travelling pack and bow fall to the ground and turned away.

Almost without thinking, I began to run blindly towards the Galloway hills, desperate to be alone... escaping from all the slaughter and carnage... distancing myself from the wretchedness of my family's final moments... this world of misery and wanton destruction.

I willed myself to run faster; to flash through the air like a swallow swooping over the lush green pastures of the Machars. As a bird I'd be free to breath the fresh untainted atmosphere, and break away from the bonds of loyalty which had kept me tethered to all this... the worst of human behaviour.

I was soon in the hills, moving upwards towards that place where I knew the spirits of my father and mother would be waiting for me.

Through my tears I glanced into the trees on either side and saw the fast running streams decked with ferns, the torrents of water crashing against outcrops of rock overlaid with rich moss, and those beautiful trees. I remembered my father's patience as he'd tried to teach me how to hunt. Glancing into the canopy above my head, I blinked through the shimmering window of moisture that clouded my view and saw shafts of light. I would soon be there... above the tree line.

Gasping for breath, I emerged from the woodland and looked upwards into the sky. The ominous cloak of darkness which had lingered over me throughout my sea crossing had been transformed into a cluster of giant ships. They were floating smoothly away, the tops of their sails dazzling in the bright sunshine. I was fantasizing... they were clouds... but it didn't matter; the shapeless hulks were helping to draw some of the grief and confusion from my frenzied mind.

I lowered my gaze towards the standing stones and began to recover my faculties... my sense of hearing and clarity of vision. I moved forward, climbed the steep grassy mound, and advanced towards one of the flanking stones. Reaching out, I ran my hand slowly down its side and felt its enduring strength.

And then I glanced out across the Solway, towards the Machars, feeling the glow of the sun as it dipped lower towards the village of Novantes. With that warmth I felt the tenderness of Apolonia's love and Ninian's guiding influence.

It would soon be evening. I would sleep here tonight alongside the spirits of my family and my ancestors; those who'd given me life. I drew a deep breath; my chest still trembling with emotion. It would take time to regain my full composure... Ninian had once said that an hour of pain was as long as a day of pleasure.

My instincts told me that I wasn't alone. I'd heard movement amongst the trees; could it possibly be...? Had I any right to hope that the spirits of my family had followed me here? I heard it again... the snap of a twig... but closer this time.

I trembled. The Druid had warned that no-one but he was entitled to meet with the dead. But surely these weren't spirits; these were real people... I could hear the rustling of their clothes. And they were very close... emerging from the forest behind me! My family had survived and were coming out of hiding to welcome me home! I spun round to greet them.

But the joy was short-lived. I was struck by a new sense of terror, more stupefying than the pain of bereavement. I was confronted by a tribe of heathen thugs... the cruel reverse of what I'd hoped to see. I knew from their faces that they were Picts. But there was something more than blue paint. They were splattered with gore... the blood of my people! I stood rooted to the spot and felt my heart pounding again. Should I make a run for it? I glanced behind. Too late! They'd encircled the stones, trapping me at the centre.

"I know you...!" I cried, my voice sounding tense and immature like a frightened child. "I've been at Cadder for the past year... I've lived with your people!"

They were strangely quiet... cold and disinterested.

I glanced around again. Where was Plebius? He must have stayed behind at the settlement. I'd been through all this before, but not without Ninian and Plebius!

Then one of the gang cried out.

"He's here...!"

Another yelled...

"We've got him cornered!"

I heard more people running through the woods. They sounded clumsy, lacking the grace and tact of good huntsmen. They burst noisily into the open behind me. Too stunned to move, I continued looking ahead... I just wanted to disappear.

"He wasn't difficult to find," someone said gruffly. "We followed him... he was blubbering like a babe!" The gang were now laughing and jeering, but I felt no shame.

There was something familiar about that wheezing sound as someone approached me from behind. And something about the way these people were holding back, as if in awe of a greatly feared leader. My heart sank lower as I felt a shroud of gloom descending over me... could it be...?

"Careful, Eingel...," someone laughed. "We haven't searched him yet!"

Suddenly, a tremendous blow between my shoulders sent me reeling. Winded, I sank to my knees, and fell forward onto my hands. This was humiliating and undeserved after all I'd been through! Without a second to draw breath I was kicked hard in the ribs, the impact rolling me onto my side. Something had broken inside my chest. I gasped for air, and braced myself for the surge of pain I knew would follow... another kick, and I'd die for sure. I looked up and saw Eingel looming over me like a misty apparition.

"He's not armed!" Eingel gurgled. He cleared his throat noisily and spat into my face. "He's just a lick-spittle chicken... tie him to the stones!"

Hauled to my feet, I drew a sharp breath... an involuntary response to the searing pain which swept across my chest. Two of the gang dragged me backwards until I felt myself flung against something hard; a flanking stone. Cords were tied around my wrists, and then my arms were stretched behind me until I was pinioned tightly with my back against the stone. I felt my ribs opening up, my breathing becoming shallow and spasmodic as I fought desperately to gain more air whilst trying not to worsen the pain. Another cord was stretched across my face, secured tightly around the stone, twisting my head sideways and pulling my cheek hard against the rough surface. I strained to look from of the corners of my eyes and saw Eingel's hideous frame. He was holding a long thin leather strap, stretching it tightly between his massive hands.

"You came home," he rasped. "Bad idea, chicken... *bad* idea...!" He began tying a knot to one end of the strap. "Your father died bravely... for a Celt." He looked up and jerked the knot tight. "They all died well; especially that little golden haired creature... what was her name?"

I fought to suppress a vision of Kaylin's final moments. Ninian said that the Christ God identifies deeply with the suffering of those undergoing torture... and that Christ Himself had shown compassion for them by dying on the cross.

Eingel was talking again.

"Not going to tell me her name...?" he smirked. "Never mind, chicken... we won't press the point... open wide now... its time for your last meal!"

Two of the gang, one on either side, wrenched open my mouth whilst Eingel plunged the knotted end of the strap down my throat.

"Swallow, or die of suffocation, chicken!" he yelled.

Gagging and choking, I gulped it down, only to be fed with more. Eventually, only the end of the strap was left dangling from by mouth.

"Good pigskin leather," he hissed with laughter. "...With our compliments!"

Through my tears I saw him moving away. They were all leaving. I was being left alone... helpless, still gagging, and almost blinded by the pain.

Could I escape? It was still possible... I'd wait until nightfall; perhaps Plebius would come. Perhaps this agony would ease... just enough to let me struggle loose. I must control the gag reflex... recover my strength. The blackness was closing in; I lapsed into insensibility.

I felt a punch on my shoulder and awoke in a daze. How long had I been unconscious? I saw something impaled in my collar bone... an arrow shaft! Then another blow to my thigh... they were shooting at me from close range! There was a sharp crack as an arrow tore through my upper arm just inches from my chest. The shaft had snapped, leaving the arrowhead wedged in the stone.

"That's enough...!" yelled Eingel. He came closer... right up to my face. "It's time to die, chicken," he whispered. Then he breathed into my ear... "Remember to say hello to the golden girl for me."

I couldn't bring myself to look at him, but knew what I was in for. The short sword... it was always to be my fate. But as I rolled my eyes to the sky I felt something tugging deep inside my throat. This was no sword... what was he doing to me? The strap in my mouth... he was pulling it tight, and the knot was caught somewhere deep inside my gut! Eingel was heaving up on my stomach and my insides were giving way!

In my panic I tried to focus on the sky. I thought of Kaylin... of Apolonia and Ninian. But I needed more... much more to quench the burning fire that raged within me. Please... Christ God...! Have mercy...! Make it quick...!

My body writhed and strained against the terrible agony, but my mind was already starting to detach itself. I began to hear music, even richer and more harmonious than the lovely strains of Drusilla's harp. In the midst of my wretchedness there came an outpouring of beautiful melody... I was floating... like a bird on a bright summer's day, and moving skywards on an endless current of warm air. I felt my eyes closing, but saw the darkness falling away to be replaced by a brilliant and all-encompassing whiteness.

I felt strong and alive again. I was leaving my tortured body behind... rising swiftly upwards towards another place... clean, radiant, and wholly free of violence.

CHAPTER 12

I soared higher, my sense of expectation stimulated by the sound of wonderful music.

Straining my eyes, I tried to focus on a misty figure dressed in white and moving across my face like an ill-defined cloud. I was about to enter the otherworld... as a bird.

Slowly, the harmonies which had brought me to the pinnacle of my upward journey began to fade and I heard the voice of a woman.

"Good..." she said, "I thought that might wake you up. Try to relax; we're almost done." Parts of Eingel's pigskin strap were still lodged in my throat; I could feel her easing out the remnants. "There... it's all over. You can breathe again."

Then I heard a man's voice...

"How's he coping?" It sounded like Plebius.

"He's waking," the woman replied. "And the tube's out."

I felt her cool hands near my temples... she was removing something from around my ears. The music stopped. I blinked, and saw her smiling down at me, her long golden hair gathered up under a white coronet. I opened my mouth to speak, but would anything come out?

"K... Kaylin...?"

My voice sounded weak and hoarse. Her face... it

was moving away out of focus. At one moment she'd been hovering over me, and the next she had disappeared.

"So... you've decided to come back to us!" The man had taken her place by my side.

He was also dressed in white, and through the haze I seemed to recognize his youthful features.

"Plebius..." I croaked.

Like me, Plebius would have been tortured to death. But he must have raced ahead as he often did... arriving before me to take his place here, in the other-world. I felt a sense of pride. I'd come through my last few hours of human suffering sharing something of Plebius's final agony.

"Take it easy, Richard... you're hallucinating." He leaned closer to my face. "Now tell me... where have you've been for the last couple of days?"

"Dying...," I murmured. It was an honest enough answer, but I felt disconcerted. Who was *Richard*?

"Oh, yes..." he went on. "You were certainly dying. And if it hadn't been for your family...?"

"Family...?"

My thoughts flashed back to Apolonia standing forlornly on her father's balcony. She was cradling our son, and watching me as I gathered up my belongings. I sensed the fresh breeze... a sudden chill... the chaotic swirling in the treetops... a stark premonition of the rough sea crossing which lay ahead. Moments later I was hastening away with Plebius; returning home to my father's settlement by the river Fleet.

"Yes... Hilary, Anna, and Michael... remember? They thought you'd had a stroke. Your wife sent the children to find help. Luckily for you, they managed to find a farmhouse... not so easy, up in those hills. You've caused quite a stir, Richard Dunstan!"

Wife, children... Dunstan? I was entering the

realms of a new but strangely familiar world; a place of order and great speed... of multitudes of people and of constructs that would put the chapels of Cadder and Novantes to shame.

This was a place where men were judged by the strength of their intellectual achievements, and where the grace of an animal's scent borne on a gentle breeze had been reduced to an irrelevance. And yet he'd mentioned the *hills*... the standing stones!

My mind opened to the vision of my wife and two children walking away from me.

"They're leaving me alone...," I gasped.

"Steady now...!" The man straightened up. "Alright... they can come in now."

"And not before time," said the woman.

I began to feel agitated. A stroke... that was serious, wasn't it? Paralysis... loss of speech... inability to communicate; I wanted to know more, but I was being abandoned again!

No... the white lady... she was still with me, fussing with my pillow. I must focus on her... see how she was dressed. A smart, smooth outfit... like a uniform... a nurse! I was in hospital. And that man... not Plebius, but a doctor!

"We can't have you looking as if you haven't been up for days."

She moved quickly around my bed, briskly smoothing the cover.

"What happened? Did I fall... hit my head... was it a stroke?"

"You really don't remember...?" she paused to look down at me. "Not even what you were eating...?"

"Eating...?"

"Think, Richard... those small, sticky things, with brown tops and pink gills."

"Loch Trool... the trout...!"

156

"Trout...?" she looked puzzled. "Where on earth have you been? No... not trout... *toadstools*!"

"Or magic mushrooms...?"

This was the voice of another woman. She swept into view and took my hand.

"You're looking a lot better," she smiled.

I knew her... she was someone very special... a companion with whom I'd already shared much of my earthly life... Hilary.

I ought to say something... anything... but I couldn't. I was fearful; poised at a threshold, and confused about my true identity. I felt an unwillingness to disengage from my Celtish roots; loath to loosen my grip on those extraordinary events which had served to illustrate our human capacity for bravery, insight, love... and terrifying evil.

I thought about Plebius's mastery of the sling... and his cool presence of mind when forced by the barbarians to demonstrate his skill whilst facing the prospect of a slow and painful death. I thought of Ninian; of his powers of gentle persuasion, his utter humility, and his astonishing ability to command attention and respect at every level of society... even so far as to win the friendship and religious allegiance of a Pictish king. And I thought of Apolonia and Kaylin, the one serene and tranquil, the other buoyant and animated... those I had loved to the very depths of my being.

"The doctor said you'd been dreaming about death," said Hilary softly, squeezing my hand.

Death...? I closed my eyes and thought of Ninian's pale thin face, and those precious moments in his company. I recalled our time together on the banks of Loch Trool where he'd told me of his yearning to continue in God's service. And not just for a lifetime, but to go on working through his spirit, seeking out the depths of human pain and anguish, bringing hope and encouragement to those weighed down by tyranny, oppression, poverty, anxiety and strife.

It had seemed impossible at the time, but now I began to understand that his influence was still being felt... and his wish fulfilled.

Death...? Not for him. The soul of that remarkable man, the legendary Bishop St Ninian, had transcended the great interval of time between us. I could still hear his gentle voice, unravelling that greatest of human mysteries...

"The important thing in life, Gaelen, is not to win every trial, but to fight it well; and to remember that death is God's last and greatest gift to the living."

Gaelen... I smiled at the name. Through Gaelen, my mind had been opened to wondrous things... to gods, warriors, and that extraordinary race of Celtic people living in the raw of nature.

But what now...? What kind of future was I moving towards? Not as a hunter like Gaelen, free to roam the glorious hills of Galloway, but as a modern man... a *Company man*? I would need to drive myself forward... meet all the challenges and overcome the inevitable disappointments... force myself to endure the vagaries of an unappreciative, egocentric and conceited board of senior managers. But *should* I? Must I allow everything that happened to Gaelen melt away?

I was being lured out of my dreamlike state by the sound of Hilary's voice.

"But what we'd *really* like to know, is where you found this."

She was pushing something into the palm of my hand.

"What is it?" I whispered, raising my head to see.

"You had it clenched in your fist when you arrived

in the ambulance... it's a bronze arrowhead. You didn't want to let go of it."

Again, I was drifting back in time. Was it really just a few days ago that I'd first taken hold of the arrowhead? It seemed more like a whole year since Hilary and the children had moved away leaving me alone at the cairn. I remembered touching the flanking stone, the scene of Gaelen's brutal end; where Pictish arrows were shot into him from close range, and where something sharp had fallen into my hand.

"It's Eingel's," I murmured.

I let my head fall back onto the pillow, tightening my grip around that beautifully crafted work of art which had contributed so much to my final agony. And then I heard a shuffling... a tug at my elbow.

"You okay now, Dad?" Michael beamed.

"I'm very much okay. What have you been up to?"

I felt a tender kiss on my cheek. It was Anna.

"Hi, Dad... we're staying on holiday until you're better!"

"I've booked another week," explained Hilary. "There's no point in hurrying back... not until you're well again."

Just one more week... and then what? Drift meekly back to work...? Return to my former self and forsake my ancestors... those whose lives had been a constant battle for survival? They'd taken me into their hearts, accepting me for what I was; neither clever nor strong, but vulnerable to criticism and self-doubt. I'd formed a deep intimacy with my Celtish brothers and sisters; they'd become part of me, and it would be senseless to pretend that I could face the future without them.

I was looking at Michael... but thinking of Callum.

"No, a week isn't enough." My voice was beginning to fail. "You can't learn precision shooting... not in a week... not in a year."

"Richard!" exclaimed Hilary. "You can't be thinking of staying!"

I remained silent, unable to think of a suitable reply as she stared at me in disbelief.

"But... but what could we do... living up here in the wilds of Galloway?"

I swallowed hard, squeezing my eyes against the burning sensation still raging at the back of my throat.

"Do...?" I looked into Michael's happy face. "Well... this young man could learn to shoot."

But I had to think about my own position. Was I ready to accept Ninian's assertion that contentment fails wherever wealth holds sway; that it's better to glory in the freshness of a labourer's dream than to worship at the shrine of luxury and pride? Yes... I *was* ready to accept it... in my heart I'd always known it to be true. But somehow I must convey as much to others... open a window into my mind so that they might see and understand my rationale.

"If only... if only I could learn to write..." I murmured. "There's a story waiting to be told."